IF CAMPFIRES COULD SPEAK

SHORT STORIES

CINDY PEREIRA

Made with ❤ on the Notion Press Platform
www.notionpress.com

Contents

Contents

I

The Ghosts of Mermaids

Freddy Merrill stared googly-eyed at the picture on his computer and licked his thick, avid lips. With a glance, anyone could tell that the original snap had been that of a fully clothed, nice-looking girl. Now, it had been sleazily morphed into the body of a very voluptuous woman, pink, full, shapely, and completely nude.

Over his computer, at the desk in front of him, the girl from the picture stood in real life, her back to him. She pulled a sheet of paper from a printing machine whose mechanical hiss sounded like a steady blow of steam in the quiet office room. Merrill grinned and licked his lips again, adjusting his thick glasses to get a better view of the unsuspecting girl's rear. Dressed in sombre black, Becky Coleman was one of those office interns who collected print-outs and carried files from one desk to the next.

A secret voyeur, very lewd and very slippery, he gazed at her rear, snug but serious in their trousers, and mentally and delectably undressed her to the sliver of a black thong! That almost brought a drool to his fat lips, and he shuddered as prickles of sweat lathered his spine and spangled across his egg-shaped body.

Middle-aged, unsightly podgy, and, to top it off, a total recluse, Merrill knew that the opposite sex barely even acknowledged his existence. But Becky Coleman here, in her all-black office attire, had smiled affably at him on her first day at work. It had given him sleepless nights, carousing with graphic magazines and visualising her sweaty and naked with him.

And oh! Her perfume drove him wild! It had the scent of an aromatic sea breeze—of beach palms and mermaid scales, of wild and remote shores, where sunsets glimmered like liquid gold on the horizon, and women in coconut shell bras gyrated around sparking fires.

Becky had befriended him despite his podgy belly protesting against his belt, his iron-grey, oily hair and his magnified eyes behind the thick 'soda bottle' glasses. Sometimes, she'd bring him a cup of coffee or a sandwich and order him to eat because she always believed he worked scrupulously on his accounts books, with his head ducked and intent in his ledgers.

"Come on, Mr Merrill," she'd say with filial affection, oblivious of the shameful truth he hid under the veneer of reserve. "I never see you taking a break."

He resembled a large egg balancing on a pair of thin legs – a total Humpty Dumpty scurrying up or down the seven floors of the office because he was utterly claustrophobic and, therefore, entirely petrified by the building lift.

He also hated to be alone in the dark and was in absolute terror of ghosts!

It might have been a laughing matter to see the egg climb up or down the stairs, heaving hard, his jowls shaking, and his thick glasses sliding down a sweaty and stubby nose, but Becky was always filled with sympathy to see the shapeless man suffer so.

"Pity that the exercise doesn't help at all," was her unspoken thought that day as she inspected the letter she had drawn from the printer, oblivious of the covetous gawps she received from behind.

A young, suited manager approached her at that moment.

"Is the letter all good?" he asked, craning his neck at the document in her hands. "Yeah, it's fine," he added after quickly reading it to ensure it was free of typographical mistakes. "Take it over to Mr. Berkley for his approval."

As she moved away, he continued, "You're sure it's okay to stay over tonight to get that done?" With his nose, he gestured to the letter. "It's Friday, and I have no right to ask this of you on a weekend."

"I'm happy to oblige," Becky replied.

"The office can get very silent and lonely after office hours, you know," he added with an eyebrow of concern.

"It isn't going to be too long," she shrugged. "It's only a matter of turning that switch, that's all. Besides, I don't live too far away."

Hidden behind his computer, Merrill grinned. With a whimsical glance at a pile of papers on his desk, he convinced himself that he also had a ton of things to do – backlogs of filing and balancing of accounts and various other things that had piled up because of his licentious diversions – what better time was today, after hours, to start some of it? Not that he was going to finish anything anyway. There was too much sleaze on his mind, and the sweet, innocent and obliging Becky talking to her young boss had come to embody all of that.

By eight that evening, the office turned silent. The winter fog had rolled in from the sea, and through the glass windows on the seventh floor, the night outside was a grey, swirling curtain punctuated by uncertain lights flickering along the street. Merrill glanced out once and shivered, hating the darkness. He peeped over his desk and looked around for Becky Coleman. Of course, she had no idea he had stayed back, too, hidden as he had been behind his desk in the corner. He rarely stayed back any later than required because of his fear of darkness. To now get over his abject dread, Merrill quickly averted his gaze back to his screen. The picture of an undressed woman illuminated his face, and he trembled. Sighing and sweating, and with an oath of despair that he could never have one like her, he shut the machine down.

At least Becky was real, he told himself. She had smiled and spoken to him, giving him one of those second glances he had never received from any other woman before. Indeed, she would also welcome his other advances.

Why the hell wouldn't she?

He'd get a coffee, he decided, and in doing so, would chat her up...perhaps feel her up, too, if he got the chance. She was tender and fawn-like, pretty and rosy, and he lusted for her, even more so because she was almost half his age. He had even stalked her home one evening and discovered with a swell of unholy glee that she was unattached and lived alone. That had led to a more promiscuous fantasy of a lovely sylph-like creature parading about her small apartment, glistening and naked after a shower.

Freddy Merrill had found it difficult to walk back home that night, and it wasn't because of the darkness!

He now rose from his chair and was momentarily stunned by the shadowy silence of the office. For an instant, his knees turned weak, and he wondered if he had made the right decision to stay back. Across and through the glass panelling, he saw a glow from a computer screen, partially obliterated by the prim and slim back of the girl he lusted for.

"Hell, yeah, it is," he told himself.

First, the men's, he thought, realising he had a full bladder. Then coffee, he decided—one for him and one for her. Maybe a drink later and... he might be the one turning switches and watching her parade about her apartment naked!

At her desk, oblivious that she was being watched with avaricious, bespectacled eyes, Becky glanced at her watch and realised it was time. The letter to Mr Berkley had been a request for his approval to shut down the building's power so that maintenance work on the electrical connections could commence over the weekend. They had planned to complete the work by Sunday evening.

Becky shut down her computer and rose, donning her thick winter coat and reaching for her handbag. She quickly scanned the floor and satisfied herself that all had left for the day. Then she checked the 'break-out' area where the coffee machine lights twinkled at nobody. Satisfied with her checks, she proceeded to the exit to inspect the remaining six floors below before shutting down the power. Her boots were soft-soled, so she almost glided across the floor as she made for the exit.

Emerging from the cloakroom, having completed his ablutions, Merrill froze as a shadow swept by him and vanished towards the floor's exit. The gust of warm air that swept across his face had a trace of sea breeze in it. It had the fresh scent of beach palms and mermaid scales and might have driven him into a sweat of desire. It didn't. The darkness, silence, and, moreover, the prickly sensation that someone had moved in the shadows froze him in a paroxysm of terror.

All that filled his mind now was the bizarre notion of wandering mermaid ghosts floating in from the sea. From the long sunken ruins of some ancient galleon and stirring from their death sleep, he imagined them washing up upon the shore, flesh dropping away from bones through which the fog penetrated like smoke from a cigarette. The hair on the back of his neck prickled. He looked down the corridor, but it was now empty, silent, and dark. Whatever the thing was, it had passed him like a whisper and had vanished!

"Hello," he hesitatingly called, his voice trembling. "Who's there?"

With a pang of terror, he charged towards the glass panelling where he had last seen Becky and fell into a cold sweat when he realised her seat was empty. Palpitating now, he hurried to his desk, grabbed his things, and ran, terror-stricken, towards the glass door, where a green light above labelled it as the exit. It opened automatically—one of those shadow-sensing doors that swung back with a dull hiss.

Running towards the steps, he struggled to take them two at a time and nearly pitched headlong. He made a hilarious sight—a strange rotund, penguin-shaped figure waddling down a stairway. Suddenly, he froze again. Further below, footfalls, movement, and a pattering of soft shoes reached his ears, and he nearly screamed in terror.

Was the 'thing' coming up the stairs again?

He hurried back up in a cold sweat, ran past the hissing door of the empty office floor, hesitated under the green exit sign and shot out into the foyer again. Below, the soft footsteps sounded nearer and nearer, and Merrill moaned in panic. With terror clutching at his stomach, turning his legs almost to jelly, he charged for the lift. Glancing over his shoulder, again and again, he repeatedly pushed the buttons as he waited for the box to slide up its shaft. It beeped as it opened before him, all lit up and welcoming. With a loud gulp, he entered and pressed the button to the ground level. He began to gasp as the doors trapped him in; then, he began to descend.

On the lower floors, Becky quickly completed her search of the building to make sure no colleagues were working late. Finally, reaching the basement, she moved towards the fuse box, opened it and pushed the lever up. The dull hush of the powerlines that emanated from the heart of the building instantly wound down to deep silence. She then buttoned up her coat, slung her bag across her body and walked home, unfazed by the thick, swirling fog.

Meanwhile, Freddy Merrill leaned back as the sickening feeling of a bad stomach flooded through him. As the lift continued its descent, he strove to breathe, heaving as his fat body threatened to explode over his belt.

"Please-please-please," he whimpered in his rising panic.

Suddenly, he jolted to a halt and plunged into terrifying blackness.

At first, he only froze.

Then he screamed, howled and banged against the walls of the lift, clawing at metal and gulping down air. Trapped in the darkness within walls that now closed him in, his stomach rumbled, churned, and threatened to let him down. He hammered against the unyielding steel, found the slit between the two doors and grunted aloud, trying to pull it apart.

It didn't yield, and with a wail of utter dismay, he sank to the floor in a sweat.

On the following Sunday evening, when the power was turned back on, the maintenance men found Freddy Merrill crumpled upon the floor of the lift, his nails bloody, and his trousers embarrassingly soiled by his faeces. Remarkably, he was still alive but wild-eyed and incoherent in his explanations.

The only word that escaped his fat, quavering lips was 'mermaids.'

Becky Coleman could never understand how Freddy Merrill came to be found lying crazed with terror in the lift.

He always used the stairs.

She was even more muddled that he was eventually placed in an institution for deranged people.

II

In'cast'cerated

I brought my husband home with his ankle in a blue cast. With his new Zimmer frame, he hopped to the sofa and sank heavily into it, sighing loudly. His ordeal was over.

Mine had started.

I'm a late riser nowadays – my battles with intermittent insomnia fade to deep sleep at the first light of dawn. When I rise, long after the sun is up, I'm irritable and moody. It's my 'lord and master' who is up early, shifting and puttering about in the kitchen, doing the dishes, making the coffee and breakfast, and being a nuisance to no one but himself.

After breakfast, I take the baton from him – it's a fair division of labour, and we are both a well-oiled, domestic machine.

At least until now!

With his leg in'cast'cerated (and that's one of the scribblings on his blue cast), the load of the hearth has fallen on my shoulders.

Today, I crawled out of bed at dawn, shivering from the nippy air, and glared at him for not waking me up earlier.

"You were fast asleep, and I didn't want to wake you," he calmly replied. You were also snoring," he added as a joke, which I didn't find funny. Being menopausal was bad enough; adding a feature like 'snore' to the existing 'snooze' to this human appliance was insulting.

"I don't snore. *You* snore," I answered like a juvenile, and my husband chuckled with manly pride.

"Like a chainsaw!"

He had tried to make us some coffee but had failed, having yet to learn the fine art of managing the Zimmer frame with one hand and the bottle of milk with the other. I firmly sat him down on the sofa and swore I would get through this.

I put my hair up in a knot and got those irritating tresses out of the way. Tresses! Looking at myself in the mirror in the mornings is a nightmare. I have to view myself in parts – first, the right side and then the left.

We could have solved that problem with a broader mirror...or with some exercise, I think dryly now.

Avoiding that reflecting surface, I hurried to the kitchen, to the coffee percolator, cleaned out yesterday's dregs, and loaded it up for a new pot of decoction. It complained, steamed (is it supposed to do that?), and eventually brewed. When I took a cup to him, he'd vanished into the toilet. With a tired sigh, I placed the cup on the kitchen top and decided to take note of the doggy whines that were emanating from the outside.

Our two dogs. Of course, they needed to be walked! They can't walk themselves! I mean, they can, but then we'd have to answer many uncomfortable questions later on, so I donned my coat and got ready to step out into the grey morning. I'm more of a cat person – for me, dogs are dogs. Cats are precious gems, babies, darling lumps, my 'puppa caats'!

I realised that these darlings were watching me intently around the kitchen door. All four of them – and they had this look that said:

"Now that you're awake, you might as well do yourself a favour and feed us!"

I crumbled with a groan. Reaching into the cupboard that holds their food, I fed each one with love. With a desultory sniff at their bowls, they walked away in disgust but, a moment later, wrapped hopefully around my legs again. Ignoring the ache forming in my back, I picked each fluff ball up and placed them before their food, coaxing them to eat. Outside, the whines persisted, and inside, the fussbudgets mocked me disdainfully. With a sigh, I gave up and left the cats to their fastidiousness.

Precious gems, babies, darling lumps, my puppa caats? Today, I didn't think so.

When I stepped outside with the walking leads, the dogs looked suspiciously at me, wondering where the master of the house was. How they had barked at him when we'd returned from the hospital! They sniffed him with suspicion, darted back in doubt, and took one more whiff at his cast, growling at him and his Zimmer frame. Finally, they nearly knocked him down with love!

He's a total dog person.

The walk took longer than expected because dogs will be dogs. Just as humans have newspapers and social media to waste time on, dogs have electric poles, car tyres, walls, trees, and even the wayside flowers to sniff and lift their legs over. With a sense of urgency, mingled with a bit of guilt because this was their time, I dragged them away from every sniff they indulged their noses in.

"Not today, you chaps," I gritted at them. "Not for the next five weeks."

When I returned, the hubby was reclined on the sofa, with pencil and paper, mulling over some scribblings that looked like a complicated trigonometry sum. I only made a face at him and vanished into the kitchen to bring him his coffee. Then I attacked the sink – because it's only the two of us, using the dishwasher is too painful. First, you've got to clean the crud off, load all the dishes in the machine, face down, and then wait two hours! I can clean that sink in half an hour flat!

I did and ended up with that terrifying ache intensifying in my lower back. Ah! I thought. Those muscles have long been rusted from all the husband pampering I've had. It's time they worked for their keep!

I also had water all over the kitchen floor, a soaked T-shirt, and a rosy, dimpled tummy sticking out underneath. I cleared the moisture immediately, lest the hubby hobbled in on some pretext. It had resulted in the blue cast in the first place – a wet floor, a slip, a struggle to save a glass of whisky, and a terrific toss. The glass of whisky had been spared, but not the ankle.

Talk about priorities! Anyway, there was no time to think of causes and effects. I start work at nine sharp, and mercifully, I work from home. The hubby had opted for early retirement to pursue his master's in mathematics, so his day is spent with radians, calculus, integers, formule and equations...and lots and lots of coffee.

"Eggs?" I asked him because that's the easiest and the fastest thing to prepare in the morning.

The hubby is never fussy. His response of "Sure thing, darling," set the process going with the skillet and the eggs. I thought this would be easy, but then he dropped the bomb!

"How about buttering up the bread and browning it a little for that added snaz!"

"Coming up."

"And perhaps bacon and beans?"

"Okay"

"How about some hash browns, too?"

I groaned softly but hopped to it.

"And some more coffee now would be great," he added.

Anything else, I asked myself, rolling my eyes. Well, I then realised. I hadn't had any coffee myself yet. It would indeed be great! So, I attacked that machine again – since we were such coffee guts, making a whole pot wouldn't be wasted. With the percolator loaded up to its maximum, I started on breakfast. The bubbling sounds from the percolator sounded like the rumbling lungs of a tuberculosis patient and the puff of steam like the snorting of a miniature black bull. When it ceased bubbling and steaming, I poured it out, and added a spoonful of sugar to mine because the hubby doesn't take sweet with his, stirred it, and ended up handing him the wrong cup. He only laughed and reached for the coffee in my hand as I took a sip.

"What a face!" he observed with a guffaw. "I suggest sugarless coffee for you, too, from now on, darling," he added outrageously, and I wanted to pitch the hot beverage all over him. Of course, if one analysed it, I had no reason to be upset. He had only paid me a compliment.

Sipping my coffee, I started on the eggs, making a mess with the shells. As I looked around for the roll of tissues to wipe my gooey fingers, the bacon flew in, frying too crisp for anyone's liking.

Hash browns—hash browns—hash browns. How are they made? Potatoes, pepper, salt...and grated fingertips.

Soon, they were sizzling, too, crumbling to pieces when I tried to flip them over. Well, my man would have to make do. It's the taste that matters, not the presentation. Besides, he's not Gordon Ramsay, and I'm not Nigella Lawson!

The bread skidded into the pan the next instant, sizzling under the blitzkrieg of the butter. Still, with my attention on the mounds of grated potato, the eggs crackling away, and the milled pepper freckling up the orange yolk, I forgot all about the overheated pan. The bread began to smoke and char, and the butter burned brown. As I flipped the slices over, biting my lips at the carbonised corners, the hubby hobbled into the kitchen.

"Don't say a word!" I warned.

"*Hmm, I like it like that,*" he crooned to Shania Twain's famous hit song and hopped to the sink with his coffee cup handle secure in the hook of his thumb. Depositing it there, he smiled at me, blew me a kiss, and limped away, the *click-clack* of the Zimmer fading away as he retreated.

When breakfast was done, which left our front teeth all blackened (and I worked my tongue overtime to bring the pearl whiteness back), it was back to the sink for me with the dishes. With the tap bubbling on my soapy hands, I gripped the China carefully because the suds were slippery. Then I heard the scraping of the Zimmer again. Closer and closer, it shuffled, and I couldn't help but wonder, albeit with a chuckle, that if this were a horror movie, my husband would have been a limping psychopath advancing second by every terrifying second to my place of concealment.

It sounded louder and louder, and with a slanted eye, I watched the kitchen door as my hands worked up a pyramid of soap suds around a cup. Then, a dark head appeared, followed by a smiling face.

"It's a quarter to nine," he announced.

"And I've got to feed the dogs," I moaned.

"Starve the bastards," he suggested with a facetious grin, and I glared at him. I might be a cat lover, but no animal goes hungry on my watch.

"Keep quiet," I retort. "Go...solve a sum!"

Half an hour later, I was at my office desk, sagging in my seat. Today was day one, I thought. Five more weeks to go! I groaned and cradled my head on my desk.

The scraping of the Zimmer sounded again, and it tapped closer, closer, closer. Finally, it came up alongside me; with my face still cradled in my arms, I only prayed that he didn't want another cup of coffee. I straightened and looked wearily at him as he bent down and gently kissed my cheek.

"I love you," he said. "You're my hero!"

I smiled and collapsed a little more in my chair with a deep sigh of fulfilment.

On the bright side, I get to hear nice things...and perhaps lose a little weight.

III

The Irregulars of St. Agnes

"Oi detectives," came a shout.

Two little girls swung around. Sadie had a heavy magnifying glass in her pocket and wore an ill-fitting deerstalker hat, flopping upon her freckled nose. The other, Lucy, dangled a large pipe – a Calabash from her lips. Though inert, Lucy wished she could load it up from a Turkish sandal and smoke as her famous hero did when he was in a 'disputatious mood.' She had been writing something in a small, black book and shoving a stubby pencil behind her ear. Not yet ten, both girls were clad in deep green school blazers with an embroidered St. Agnes' School emblem under their collars. A white, pleated skirt danced two inches above knotty, muddy knees; socks blossomed like cream flowers around little ankles.

Upon hearing the shout, the children froze to attention. Out from the corner, two seniors appeared. Both were tall, towering over the younger girls, and already sprouting all

the curves of early womanhood. They were also the school champions in hockey, basketball, and track. Terrors to most, every girl of every lower grade shrank from them in awe, dismay, and dread.

As the seniors neared, Lucy and Sadie braced themselves. Suddenly, the deerstalker made Sadie uncomfortable. It was too big; she had to tip her head back constantly. Snatching it off, she shoved it into her lunch bag. Lucy thrust the Calabash into her pocket, fidgeting and biting her bottom lip in anxiety. Getting cornered by two seniors was the last thing any junior wanted.

The big girls approached them, took in their small frames with one disparaging glance, and grinned, their jaws working non-stop around chewing gum.

"Still the nosy parkers?" asked one with a tone that dripped with mockery. She flicked Sadie's nose to get her to look up.

"And still make detailed reports on your letterheads?" The other asked. The guffaw that accompanied the question got both the little girls cringing. "With words that will make anyone fly to their dictionaries?"

The seniors flapped their arms and broke into peals of laughter. The two children went red.

"We have an assignment," one finally said. She plucked the pencil from Lucy's ear and examined it. "Think you two are up to it?"

The young sleuths puffed their chests out.

"Right," said the girl, trying hard not to laugh. "We will expect your report in two days."

Sadie and Lucy nodded, wide-eyed. Deep inside, both girls wanted to shout and scream with joy. Until now, the only cases they handled were missing water bottles, lost books, and misplaced pencil boxes – articles not stolen but made to appear so by well-meaning classmates. Having two seniors ask for their help was out of this world!

The big girls pointed to the school gate ahead, and one of them said:

"If you wait here long enough after the last bell, you will see one short, fat man with 'soda bottles' standing across the road. You'll have to look out because sometimes he's hidden behind the tree."

The sleuths turned and followed the direction of the pointed hand.

"Your task is simple," continued the senior, crunching her gum. "Watch him and document all that you see."

"But...but..." Sadie stammered. "But what's he done?"

"Bad things," the other girl replied, followed by a giggle. "Two days," she added as both turned to leave. We'll meet here the day after tomorrow and make sure to have your report."

The stubby pencil went flying into the bushes lining the wall.

Lucy gulped and glanced nervously at her friend as the two seniors sauntered away, their shoulders bobbing with laughter.

"I think it's a lie," she said, shaking her head. "No one in class takes us seriously. Why would these seniors?"

"What do you mean?" Sadie glanced back, perplexed. "We found the pen, didn't we?"

"Really? You think it was ever stolen?" Lucy shook her head. "Come on, let's..."

When she turned around, she gasped, standing rooted for a moment. Sadie turned too and wondered, glancing at her friend and then at the gate.

"Luce?" she asked. "What? Oh! My!" she gasped too. "Would that be the short, fat man with the 'soda bottles?'"

Donning her deerstalker again with a professional snap, Sadie hurried to the gate.

Lucy followed, whipping out her black book and fumbling for another pencil in her satchel.

Upon reaching the gate, the girls realised that this was, indeed, the man the seniors had commissioned them to investigate. He stood across the road in the shadow of the tree and looked shifty in his thick 'soda bottle' spectacles. Ducking behind the bark each time an adult approached, something about him put Lucy and Sadie on guard. Meanwhile, glancing left, right and straight at the girls, the man licked his fat lips and never once blinked. The girls wondered as they watched him. Despite the uncomfortable and fidgety demeanour, he slowly raised a hand and beckoned them.

"He's calling us, Luce!"

"Don't go!"

"No," agreed Sadie. "Let's watch him from here."

"Should I take notes?"

"Of course! They want a report, remember?"

"Okay."

"Subject stands with hands to his side, as if sleepwalking."

"Sleepwalking?"

"Sleep standing!" Sadie seethed. Did Lucy always have to get so fussy? "He has a fat face with thick, black-rimmed glasses. His eyes look round and small behind them. Ugh! I don't like his face – don't write that. Luce! He's calling us again."

"Don't bother."

The next instant, Sadie gasped, snapping her head around towards Lucy. The odd silence got Lucy to look up from her note-taking. She gawped once at her friend, then at the 'subject' across the road, and swallowed a horrified scream.

"What!"

The man now had a rubbery smile plastered across his face, and his piggish eyes never once blinked. But down below, his hand had smoothly raised his shirt lapel to expose an open fly and body parts the girls had never known to exist on a man.

They had younger brothers, officiously assisted their amused mothers in changing diapers, and enjoyed bath time with rubber ducks floating all around. Their baby brothers were such little dolls, angels – huggable and kissable. This man was swollen, red and...weird!

Shocked, the girls blinked at one another. Then they burst into hysterical laughter.

"Does it look like that?" Lucy breathed, obvious revulsion mixed with amusement on her face.

"My brother's doesn't," the other replied dubiously, her cheeks red with mirth. "What about yours?"

"No way!" Lucy exclaimed, having all the affection in the world for her baby brother. "Do you think our subject's sick?"

Shrugging in astonishment, Sadie turned again to the man across the road.

Despite the absurdity of it all, her heart raced. Her instinct warned her that whatever was happening now was not right. It went against all that her parents and teachers had taught her. Even Lucy felt uncomfortable with the man googling at them from across the road and licking his lips. His fly was still open, and his body remained displayed to the little girls. He beckoned to them again and pointed to his crotch, turning down his lips to make a sad but hopeful face.

"Maybe you're right," Sadie finally muttered. "It looks weird – all swollen and red as if he has..."

Miss Lynch, the Catechism teacher, approached the gate, noticed the man, and charged at him with a howl of disgust and anger, her handbag swinging. The little girls watched him take off down the road and disappear around a bend.

"How weird!" mused Lucy as the furious lady huffed and puffed back to them.

"Heavens!" she panted. "What's this world coming to?" Turning to the bewildered girls, she demanded, "Did that disgusting flasher hurt you?"

The children gaped at each other and then at her, confused. They shook their heads, and the woman sighed in relief. "Are you waiting for your parents to pick you up?"

Again, the girls shook their heads. They usually walked home together.

"We live down the street, Miss," Sadie explained.

"Come," said Miss Lynch firmly. "I'll walk home with you two. There's no way I'm leaving you girls alone with a pervert in the neighbourhood."

Pervert? Flasher?

New words.

Once more, the girls glanced at each other and, giggling shakily, started for home, walking on either side of the adamant teacher.

Two days later, the seniors received the report. It had a hand-drawn emblem of a deerstalker hat and a Calabash within a magnifying glass in the top left corner. The words, The Irregulars of St Agnes, encircled the symbol.

Stamped with a date, it bore a heading, '*The Case of the Man at the Gate*' and ran thus:

"*The Irregulars of St. Agnes were called upon to investigate a man standing across our school gate. The subject had a fat round face, wore thick glasses and was quite shabbily dressed. He had not tucked in his shirt, and his pants were open. Yet, he didn't seem to know or mind that he was showing off all the things we usually keep covered. So, while we laughed then because it looked funny, we now conclude that the subject has serious problems.*

"Since cameras are not allowed in school, we have drawn a picture of him for you."

The report displayed an image of a man under the tree with his shirt lapels hanging loose. The seniors noted that the Irregulars had not sketched any other details and sighed in relief.

In awe, they continued reading the report: *"The man likely has a mental problem because he could not stop smiling. We are sure about this because crazy people smile a lot.*

"But we noted something more serious. Most people are embarrassed to display their private parts, but it was apparent that this man had no other option. His privates were swollen so severely that his pants would never have zipped up.

"Considering all the facts and discussing the matter, we conclude that the man has a medical problem. This drawing will illustrate:"

A second sketch of two legs followed. One foot appeared normal in size, and the other depicted a swollen ankle. The girls enhanced the view by drawing tiny dashes around the part representing the swelling.

"As in the case of the swollen foot, a shoe will only worsen matters. So also, in this man's case, zipping up his pants would have been very uncomfortable.

"Swellings can be caused by any injury – a wound or a bump. We know if you hit a boy in his private parts, he will be very hurt and unable to stand for some time. Still, we are sure this is not that kind of wound because this man appeared fine

otherwise.

He didn't seem to have any problem when he ran.

"Swellings can also be caused by more serious internal problems, like tumours or growths. The most common tumours are cancers, which can become very serious if not treated in time.

"We conclude that the subject does not need detectives. He needs two doctors – one to treat his swelling and the other to treat his head.

"Postscript: Our investigations were cut short by Miss Lynch, who chased the man away, calling him words like 'pervert' and 'flasher.' We looked them up but could not understand the dictionary. Our parents did not help either. They said those were adult words, especially 'flasher.'"

"We thank you for using our services and hope to be of assistance again."

With this, the report ended, and the seniors broke into laughter. They reread the account and guffawed once more. But their humorous outburst had no heart, was forced and resulted in painful throats.

"They write well," observed one.

"They take their hobby seriously," shrugged the other, chewing her gum with greater vigour.

"Let's grab something to eat?"

"Absolutely! I'm starved."

Having no further need for the account, they rived it into tiny bits and sent the fragments into the air like a shower of snowflakes. Noisily chewing their gum, they looped their arms together and exited the school gate. But deep down, neither dared to admit to the other that they felt small...smaller than two ten-year-old kids.

The Irregulars of St. Agnes were now ambling ahead of them. Under a large deerstalker, one peered at something through a magnifying glass on a light pole. The other whipped out her black book, pulled a pencil from behind her ear, and took notes with a professional air, an inert Calabash hanging from her lips.

IV

Melody's Tune

The narrow lane appeared greasy under the yellow, hazy streetlights and a steady drizzle of rain. One hunched-up figure picked his way along the side, avoiding the puddles of dirty, opaque water. The pavements on either side were under repair for several weeks, so the culverts were open to the sky and a death trap! The street remained inaccessible to hapless lodgers except for plywood boards that served as make-shift bridges from closed doors over the drain. Once over this temporary crossing, folks were compelled to walk the edge of the lane, mercifully devoid of traffic at this late hour. Even more merciful was the length of this creepy pathway. It ran no more than four hundred metres from start to end, serving only as a back lane to the main street running parallel to it. That broad duct of commerce had been elevated to the esteemed position of a 'one-way' due to the sheer flow of traffic during business hours.

The figure picked its way along, avoiding the puddles. Still, an observer would have commented that the care didn't help much, for in circumventing one little body of water, the man inadvertently stepped into another.

He swore under his hat. It wasn't a very nice word, but it wasn't a pleasant evening or place either. Pulling his coat collars around his neck, he jerked his head from left to right, looking for something or someone. His face was plump; rosy nasolabial folds bulged right down to marionette lines, giving off the impression of an aged dog. Yet, he wasn't old – fifty-five could never be considered old unless the judgement belonged to one no more than fifteen. The thin, stiff lips, downturned and almost scowling, glistened with the moisture from the rain; one would have thought that this man was a mean customer, and they would not have been far from the truth. Even so, the black eyes, watery, uncertain and searching, rolling about over the puffy, pink bags, also suggested an alcoholic.

Seth Parrish was, indeed, one, although tonight, despite being soaking wet, he was 'dried out' and alert. Knowing that he needed his wits about him on this nocturnal mission, he had stoutly abstained. He was looking for an address; the paper he had scribbled it on was long since flung away because it had turned soggy, and his handwriting had smudged. But he remembered it the same way an alcoholic remembers where he hides his stash.

With a scowl, he recalled his cantankerous sister watching him with small, black, beady eyes as he donned his coat and hat and set out earlier that evening. She was much older than him, retired and contented with her single life.

"Forsythe," she had called, shoving a slip of paper into his hand. "This fell from your pocket. Thought it was money, but it turned out to be trash, like you, Forsythe!"

When she repeated the name, her eyes gleamed in their sockets, and Seth froze, ground his teeth, and turned around.

"Don't call me that," he snarled, snatching the paper from her.

That was the address he now hunted for.

"The old witch," he muttered through clenched jaws. "The old miserly witch! The sooner she..."

He plodded into a puddle and swore as a body of ditch water, about the volume of his shoe, splattered across his face.

"Aaagh!" he cried and rubbed his eyes, grimacing and spitting a few grains of mud from his mouth. At least he had by-hearted the address, he thought. He looked around on either side of him. Beyond the yawning culverts, the black windows, barred and gauzed, shone uncertain rectangles of dull light onto the greasy road.

A wonky vinyl of ancient music scratched through one. A child bawled through another. Silence floated from yet another, and a husband swore at his wife from one more.

Seth stumbled on, still looking up at door numbers and wiping his face under the onslaught of the rain. Then, when he came to the end of the lane, he turned around, perplexed. Had he missed his destination? He walked back the way he came, now scanning the row of gloomy doors and windows on the other side.

The rain came down heavier, and he could hear the water rushing like an angry monster in the open ditch, spewing towards a larger storm drain and from thereon to a morass twenty-five miles away. He shuddered – not from cold, for it was a warm, rainy night, but from the mad, slivering surface of the rushing chasm. Besides, without a drop of drink in him, he began to feel the effects of withdrawal. Why did it appear that faces were watching him from the gauzed windows? As if shadows were creeping in those mysterious hovels, swaying to wonky music and whispering to him? He shook his head to clear it and commanded himself to focus.

The sound of the rain clattered like dancing skeletons on a rooftop ahead. It pelted off the greasy puddles on the lane like miniature water explosions and hissed like a furious serpent seeking freedom in the trench. Down, his feet sloshed in their shoes, and he grimaced.

That's when he heard the sound.

"Psst!" it said again, and his head snapped around. At a black door which now opened to an even darker interior, Seth saw her standing, a slim figure draped in red, the cherry light of a cigarette glowing at her fingers. A precarious board of plywood bridged the gap between the door and the road, and she stood upon it, unmindful of the raging flood of water in the drain below.

"You must be Jack Smith?" she asked, but there was a smirk in her voice.

Seth parted his thin lips to deny it but recalled he had given her the name on the phone. So, his negative head shake and affirmation of, "That's correct—are you Melody Lyons?" were obvious contradictions.

She smiled, flicked the cigarette into the torrent and turned inside, bidding him enter the dark mystery of her abode.

Seth Parrish grimaced again. He didn't like how the cigarette hissed dead and vanished in a split second. Somehow, the hissing reminded him of his sister—her taunts, jibes, and insults—her boxes and boxes of cash, jewels, and valuables, and his own craving to be rid of her.

Picking his way, he tested his weight on the plywood board, mindful that if he fell into the ditch, it was wide enough to sweep him away to an eternity of dirt.

"It's taken heavier men," Melody said from inside. "Come in and close the door. And please remove your shoes and socks," she added authoritatively. "I can't have the muck from the road dirtying my carpet."

The room he entered was small and dark, devoid of furniture except a coat rack and a hat stand. He ignored both but removed his shoes and socks, placing the sodden articles in a corner. His heart picked up, and his mouth went dry. Melody Lyons was lovely, shapely and young. There had been girls like her years ago – not that he dated them, but his stealthy voyeurisms with a telescope gave him his kicks and much-desired release – until his sister caught him gaping into one, put two and two together and broke his instrument!

"You pervert!" she had cried.

He swore. Why did that old bat always come back to haunt him? Why did their father have to die, and why did she have to get all his wealth? How could someone so old still live like she would never die? How?

Seth Parrish then stepped into a room tainted red and furnished with a thick carpet; it soothed his wet toes and shot a ripple of pleasure around his heels. The ceiling was high – in the centre twirled, desultorily, an ancient fan, very ornate and very ineffective, for though the rain pelted down, the night's heat was oppressive. A red sofa stood against the wall. Before it, on a tiny table, a bottle and two glasses almost made him forget the girl. She now sat on the sofa, thighs one over the other, showing a length of smooth white skin where it vanished under the tight red dress.

Everything looked rosy—or was it the light in the room? Even her pretty hands, patting the couch and inviting him to sit and partake of the drink, appeared red.

He stumbled forward and flopped on the edge, glancing first at her legs and then at the bottle.

"I hope you didn't have too much difficulty finding my place," came the platitude as she offered him a cigarette, which he declined. With a shrug, she lit up and blew a cloud of smoke to the ceiling. Seth could only marvel at the full crimson lips and the smudge of the cosmetic on the cigarette filter.

"No...no," he lied with a scowl, not because he didn't like the idea of lying. Lying was his area of expertise, for it is a skill honed and refined by most alcoholics. Only the memory of the grimy road with its many dark, oily puddles deepened the marionette lines and pronounced the frown. He longed for a drink.

Divining his thoughts, Melody, with the cigarette hanging at her lips, leaned forward, picked up the bottle and uncorked it.

"So," she began. "How do you want to do this?"

"Slowly. Very slowly," came his leery growl.

With the cigarette still wafting a thin coil of smoke to the crimson-tainted ceiling, Melody poured two drinks. Offering him a glass, she raised it to her lips and inhaled deeply but didn't drink immediately.

The drink was too tempting for Seth Parrish. The aroma lifted off the surface like ambrosia wafting into his nostrils.

"I could have a drink to happier times," he stated with a travesty of a smile. The folds under his nose bulged his cheeks like two florid lemons, and sharp little teeth shone in the warm light of the room. "I'm not a drinker, you know," he lied, clearing his throat.

Melody's eyes narrowed, and a look of loathing spanned her lovely face. Still, she shrugged casually and watched him raise the glass to his lips.

"To success!" he hooted. With a tilt of his big, balding head, he tossed down the alcohol in one gulp, and his eyes gleamed. Glancing at the bottle and the consenting tilt of her head, he poured himself another liberal shot.

"You like your drink," observed his host with a drawl. "It kills, Mr Parrish."

"Then it's mighty slow," he chuckled, appearing unmindful of the name she had used. "What methods do you employ," he asked as the second drink went down enthusiastically. He poured a third round and inclined his head towards the bottle. "Good stuff. Excellent stuff." Fired by the alcohol, he leaned forward and placed his hand suggestively on her thigh. "Do you do it yourself or have others in your employment? Not that I'm particular." The drink appeared to loosen his tongue, and he rambled on. "I was never particular about anything, but yes..." he raised his hands, palms out. "As I said, it must be slow...and clandestine...sort of. I have a reputation to keep...you know what I mean?"

"Discretion is my second name, Mr Parrish."

"Good, good."

"Can I ask why?"

"Why?"

"Why do you want your sister dead?"

"Why wouldn't I," he asked truculently as the third drink went down his throat and to his head. "She's old, and she's rich. By rights, half the fortune she has is mine, but my father left it all to her."

"Didn't she also have a job with the Intelligence all her life and is now retired?"

"Exactly," grated Seth Parrish. "And draws a fat pension too!"

"Hasn't she earned it?"

"Not my inheritance. No!"

"Why did your father leave it all to her?"

"Because he was a bastard," came the grinding reply.

"And do you work?"

"Work?" he asked, almost amazed that someone could ask him such a question. "Work? Yeah! I dabble in art...stuff. You could say I'm self-employed," he added with an air of arrogance.

"Ah! One of the luckier ones, hmm?"

"Well," he drew a breath through his teeth and tried to keep it cool, but he felt his heart pick up, and a wave of nausea enveloped him. "Well, I could do with a little dough to spend."

"Your half of the inheritance?"

"Something like that... is it me, or is the room stuffy?"

Melody chuckled, laid her untouched drink on the table and rose, swaying her hips to the door. She peeped outside, surveyed the rain and raging culvert beneath her shoes and sauntered back to her seat.

"Well, Forsythe," she said and sat beside him again. Despite his wobbly head and tight chest, he stared aghast at her.

"My name is...name is..." he had forgotten the name he had given her.

"Forsythe Parrish?" offered the woman.

"W..what? How?"

"You offered me a thousand for the hit," she drawled and lit up another cigarette. "Your sister paid me double – in cash – but only on the condition that you wanted to go ahead with your sickening plan."

"B..but how did she...?" In a flash, Seth Parrish recalled his sister giving him the address as he left the house. "My God!" he croaked. "She was on to me! She knew!"

"She was in the Intelligence, you bonehead!" came the arch reminder. Melody glanced at her watch. "It won't be long now, Forsythe."

Seth gaped at her as realisation dawned. She hadn't touched her drink. He had had at least three generous shots. Reflexively, he rose with a scream and tried to charge to the door, but even as he took a step, he swooned and collapsed, gasping as his chest knotted agonisingly.

"You bitch," he gasped as his throat tightened and his tongue went thick. "What have you done to me?"

"Didn't I tell you alcohol kills?" came her distant, silky voice. "Robin!" he scarcely heard her call as he writhed and gasped at her feet. "Robin!"

A giant of a man entered through a side door and grunted at the figure twitching in dying gasps on the carpet. "You know what to do. And don't forget his shoes and socks."

A second grunt confirmed that Robin understood his mistress. He waited till Seth Parrish went still and then cleaned his pockets of all papers. Lifting the form like a rag doll, the gargantuan man tossed it into the raging drain. In seconds, the torrent took the body away like a feather in a gale. Seth Parrish's footwear followed soon after.

Melody Lyons only snuffed her cigarette and emptied the whiskey laced with sodium cyanide into the hissing tide. The empty bottle suffered the same fate, too. Then she shut her door and commented to her mute lackey:

"This is one hit that won't keep me awake at night, Robin. Go to bed now."

Seth Parrish's corpse floated into the morass two weeks later, but its identity was anybody's guess.

V
Sleep Talking

I was sweating and shivering at the same time, and Mike stared concerned at my face.

"Carlie, it's only a dream," he reasoned. "A dream. That's all."

His breath was funky, and the few tousled hairs on his balding head made him look hilarious—no, disgusting! I had to make it seem that my dream was making me grimace.

"It seemed so real,'" I exclaimed. "I heard the sound of the shovel, his grunts as he dug, and I saw him fling you in. You were limp, Mike, and bleeding from the head."

It was awful to lie to Mike. But as the case was, it might have been more terrible if I told him the truth. I had a habit of talking in my sleep, which Mike always laughed at and commented about the following day.

Last week, he brought the topic up at breakfast.

"What did I say," I asked, panicked.

"No clue at all. Only slurred words, little screams, moans and groans, as though you were in a terrific fight or ...." He broke off with a sly grin.

"Or ...?"

"Lifting heavy weights," he replied with a flippant laugh. "Playing tennis! Having sex!"

I could have killed him that day for guessing so accurately.

But tonight, I woke up to find Mike gaping at me, worried and, at the same time, quite merry. Mike was always an easy-going man – a good sort of person under the utterly unattractive exterior. Utterly unattractive of late, I must add, because he had been handsome enough when I married him five years ago.

"You were dreaming of Jeff?" he asked with a good-natured grin. "It seemed like you were having one heck of a fight. It's bad enough that you can't see eye to eye with your boss in real life. You're now dreaming of fighting with him?" he added, laughing.

"Awful dream," I said with a shiver, and it felt like cotton in my mouth. "Oh! Mike. It was such a bad dream."

"Tell me," he asked solicitously. "What did he do?"

"Oh, Gosh! What did he do?" I echoed, wondering where – how to start. Quickly, I added, "I had come home from work late in my dream, and the house was in darkness. I wondered where you were, and I called out." The story began to tumble out like verbal diarrhoea. "Then I heard sounds out back, and I went to check. I saw Jeff, and he was digging a pit."

"A pit?"

"Yes. Then you came out and tried to stop him, and both of you fought terribly and came to blows."

"Oh My!" he tossed his head back, and his bellow of laughter was like a gust of stale wind. "This is so interesting, Carlie. I love your dream. Did I win?"

His laughter was now getting to me. I had to burst his balloon. "He picked up the shovel and knocked you out."

"Oh! It's getting better," Mike's shoulders shook, and his man breasts jiggled. I thought of Jeff, my new boss – tall, strong, intent, and packed with hard muscle. Mike was no match to him – in looks or fitness.

"And then he buried you." I covered my face with my hands and shook. Poor Mike, I thought. I wish I could tell him every little bit about my dream, but he would be appalled. "I saw him bury you."

"It's only a dream," Mike replied and petted my head as if I were a small, frightened girl. "A dream, Carlie. That's all. Don't worry about it."

"I saw him bury you, Mike," I cried. What else could I say? I had to explain my moaning and groaning. "I tried to fight him, but my hands were heavy, and he was so big and strong!"

"All your arguments in the office are playing on your mind," he answered. "You know, dreams are something like a mirror to real life."

Of course, Mike was right. He was always so reasonable.

I shivered and burrowed deep under the covers. I thought of Jeff and felt my heart race. Turning over to the other side, I curled up. Mike rubbed my shoulders, and I felt his paunch against my back.

"Shhh," he soothed. "It's only a dream. I'm here, alive and well, and certainly not buried."

And he gently held me to him – my sweet, loving husband. But was that enough?

My breathing returned to normal, and though still rolled up tight, I had calmed down. Mike then kissed my cheek, leaned over and switched off the light.

"Good night, my dreamer," he said fondly. "I hope your next dream is of us making love."

I started at his words. I was happy the lights were out because I knew my face was burning with guilt.

My husband was asleep in seconds and snoring like a chainsaw beside me. My dream had shattered all slumber from my mind. Besides, with the guttural snots and growls emanating from the lump of flesh next to me, there was no way I would fall asleep. I eased out of bed, paced to the window and lit a cigarette.

Outside, the night was calm and soothing, and I sat down to look at the stars.

My phone buzzed on the bedside table, and I glanced at the incandescent screen in the darkness. Recognising the name, I snatched the phone up and ran from the room.

"Jeff," I seethed. "I told you not to call this late. What if Mike finds out?"

"I miss you," his deep, sexy voice said.

I giggled and shuddered with excitement. "We ought to give us a break for a little while," I suggested lamely. "Oh, Gosh! What an erotic dream I had of you. I was talking in my sleep too, and you know, making all those sounds, and then I woke to find Mike gaping at me."

Jeff asked a question, and I giggled even more.

"I told him I saw you burying him, that's all."

"I might do that soon," Jeff replied, and I chuckled.

What a great idea!

VI
When Angels Come Calling

The morning was muggy. Though it was still quite early, and the sun's rays were as soft as angel feathers, the heat hung like a heavy curtain of oppression.

Natalie Morris had risen late. Rising early and being 'up and about' were difficult. She was getting on, and when she opened her eyes, the fatigue never helped.

She was somewhat large, evidenced by fat accumulated around her tummy over the last two years. The grey flecks in her thick dark hair were proof of battles fought and won, and her eyes were expressive, dark and still hopeful.

Outside, a strange gust of wind kicked up. She hardly noticed it, feeling her chest tighten. As the wind ballooned the curtain like a wave and dropped capriciously, Natalie fought with a spasm of air hunger that overwhelmed her.

Her breathing came in short gasps, and her lungs felt sucked dry like a deflated balloon. At the back of her head, she knew it would release soon, but the panic that stormed inside her quickened her pulse. A friend had told her to think of the attacks as visitations from an angel – a touch of the divine to make her stronger. It was a touch alright, Natalie mused, as a wave of heat enveloped her. In seconds, trickles of sweat poured down her back and ribs, and she closed her eyes in a feeble attempt to meditate. Shuddering chills followed as if someone had emptied a bucket of ice over her. Normal, she told herself. Very normal. It was one of those terrific menopausal hot flushes that worsened with the summer heat. She counted to ten, then another ten as her heart raced and her nose felt clogged with blood.

It passed, and Natalie heaved a sigh of deep relief. Her lungs filled again like the curtain, and she yawned repeatedly. That was the sign that things were returning to normal—yawn after yawn after yawn and tears filling her eyes.

"Thank you, God," she said. "If this is what an angel's touch feels like, I shudder to think what a demon would do!"

She lived alone with two cats that vied for her attention and hated the sight of each other. Three years ago, her husband had left her for a younger woman, and since then, Natalie had been on her own.

"There's hope," she told herself, thinking of her broken life. "I will be happy someday."

Someday.

Her eyes filled with a rush of tears. Unlikely, was her next thought. She was only a wreck of a crazy cat lady now.

Avoiding one that wrapped himself around her legs, she threw on a pair of shorts and dragged herself to the kitchen to fix some breakfast.

"Angels," she thought. "I must remember the angels next time."

❦

Outside, on the street in front of Natalie's home, in the temperamental blasts of strange breeze, a tiny old man, sunken-faced and very white of hair, stumbled by. His oversized shirt, patched in several places, resembled a chessboard of faded colours. His trousers, rolled up to knotty calves, were grimy and held by a chord that passed for a belt. He carried a tattered bag containing only a large Coke bottle filled with water. It weighed the ragged bag down and threatened to snap the handles. Stretching perpendicular to his shoulder was a thin, long and flexible wooden pole – fore and aft ends bouncing as he walked. A cleaner of gutters, the old relic was the one person the world grimaced at, decried, and yet turned to when their drains packed up. But nowadays, work was scarce. With the big machines coming in, gutters were cleaned faster and without the putrid odours accompanying open manholes.

The gusts of wind almost teetered his sparse frame. Despite the disreputable bouncing pole and the tattered bag, his baggy shirt, rippling in those strange blasts, gave him an ethereal appearance. The patchwork of faded colours shimmered, and his white hair almost glimmered blue.

As he passed Natalie's gate, he turned to the curtain ballooning inward in her window. With sharp, piercing eyes ringed by a weird blue—the tell-tale symptom of cataracts, which evidently he didn't have – he noticed a silhouette sitting on her bed.

Glancing down at his disgraceful attire and the trousers rolled under his knees, he told himself there was a one-in-a-million chance of bumming a little breakfast. People shooed him away like he was a pest of disease and dirt. He glanced again at his tattered self and shrugged. He couldn't look any worse, and that's the way it was.

Perhaps this was that one-in-a-million chance?

Through the window, he saw the silhouette rise and disappear from his sight and reasoned that the lady of the house was proceeding to the kitchen. So, lowering the bag and laying the thin pole along the wall, the old white-headed relic swelled his lungs and called out.

❧

Down that same lane, standing before his shaving mirror, Gabriel Jennings scraped off a bristle around his peppery French beard. He lived alone in an apartment he had shifted into not a month earlier, having long since moved on from an ex-wife who divorced him, citing irreconcilable differences. Now, he was naked and wet, angling his face against the mirror so he could get that perfect shave. He told himself that shaving while showering saved time and softened a tough beard. His 'prim and propah' ex-wife had never appreciated the behaviour, shielding her eyes whenever she sighted his lean, hard buttocks.

"Oh! For heaven's sake, Gabe," she'd say with consternation. "Wrap a towel around yourself."

"Darling, can I not be free in my own home?" he'd laugh. "Besides, I'm saving time, see?"

He and the one he called Darling never lasted. Gabe was grateful she didn't bring up her pet peeve of his shaving in the buff before the desultory magistrate, but she stripped him of every penny he had, including the house and had said goodbye.

"Well," he thought, glancing at his reflection with a sanguine smile as he scraped the lather off, "she couldn't take your job, so that's something."

That thought hurried him up. It was getting late, and with a strange breeze howling outside, it seemed like it would rain. He rinsed his face, checked the edge of his French beard, found it satisfactory, and finished his shower.

As he towelled off, he wondered if Darling had also cleaned him out of his umbrella.

"Nah," he muttered. "Such an old-fashioned thing would hardly have suited her ladyship's refined tastebuds. It's got to be hanging behind the door."

It was.

⊗

"Gosh!" exclaimed Natalie, feeling the heat of the morning. "I wish it would rain."

Filling a mug of flour into a bowl, she began to knead with expertise when a loud hail shook the silence of her home and scattered her cats from her feet.

"Who on earth is that?" she wondered aloud, wiping her sticky hands and running to the door.

The wind picked up again and whistled through the leaves of the trees lining her compound wall. When she opened the door, a blast of hot air almost suffocated her, but the old, tattered figure by the gate, fighting the breeze, captivated her. His shirt flapped like a furled flag, and his white hair flattened against his head.

"Salaam," he said and joined his hands, paying obeisance. Then, a toothless grin spanned his face as he gestured to his mouth and stomach. "Anything will do, Madam," he begged. "Just a little to take me through the morning."

Natalie only gaped for a second. A hot wave burned across the back of her neck, down her spine and dissipated over her body like a shaft of smoke racing to freedom through a thin pipe. She gasped, her heart sinking in dread because she hated the air hunger. It made her anxious. Her chest tightened, and an urge to breathe deeply consumed her. Gulping, she raised her shoulders in a breath she knew would hurt, would only go as far as her throat and no further.

"Don't suck in all at once," a little voice deep inside her head advised. "Take it in slowly. Think of it as if it's a valve. Too fast in will only shut it and make you feel like a deflated balloon. Calm down. Know this will end. Breathe in little by little, and your lungs will fill."

Stunned for a second because those thoughts were like a strange voice in her head, Natalie closed her eyes and obeyed. She drew a breath in and ceased the intake at the first hint of tightness. She resumed it the next second and realised that wherever those thoughts came from, she was now beginning to feel a wave of relief as her lungs filled. When she opened her eyes again, sated by the fresh oxygen boost in her veins, the old man was still staring at her, hopefully, his blue-ringed eyes bright with mystery. The wind dropped, and the morning turned clear. It was still muggy, but the sky was blue, and the sun shone like gold. Natalie smiled for the first time that morning, and the old man's toothless grin widened. She opened the gate and pointed to the garden bench.

"Sit," she gestured, and he hesitated. Most people pointed to the floor when they wanted to be generous. "And wait," she added.

Running around her confused cats, Natalie revelled in a burst of energy firing her blood. The fatigue had vanished. It was the trick, she realised with a relieved sigh—the trick of beating the air hunger.

"I hope it works on the next attack," she thought as she worked away at breakfast. "The poor old sod," came her next thought, thinking of the strange old man with eyes that looked like the rings of Saturn. "The breeze will whisk him away if he doesn't eat. But how strangely it blows this morning!"

❧

With a plate heaped with breakfast in one hand and a cup of coffee in the other, Natalie fed her strange guest. She watched him polish the food with gusto, and her eyes filled with tears of pity. Observing his sparse frame, it was evident that having even a square meal was difficult for him. And to work at this age? This was the age when you put your feet up on your back porch and looked back with pride on a life well lived. Her eyes teared up some more at the thought that it was unlikely she would have any of that back porch stuff – only a pair of warring cats and loneliness.

Swallowing hard, she left the old man with his food and vanished indoors to finish her cooking. When another loud hail sounded, she returned to the door to find the man smiling in contentment.

He joined his hands once again and said:

"Thank you, Madam. I'll never forget your kindness. If you ever have a blocked drain..."

Natalie laughed and shook her head. If she did, how would she ever contact him?

He exited the gate, picked up his long pole, and walked away with a wave that looked like a blessing, his blue-ringed eyes gleaming mysteriously. A second later, Natalie realised he had left his tattered bag behind. Snatching it up, she hailed out to him and ran down the street, but the strange old man had inexplicably disappeared. As she glanced left and right on the road, the peculiar wind picked up again and brought a sudden blast of rain with it.

Natalie stood in it bewildered. Then, leaving the decrepit bag by the side, hoping he would return for it, she turned around to charge home. At that moment, she slipped, went sprawling and lay gasping on the warm tarmac, blinking at the sky from where the rain pelted down.

"Why me, God?" she yelled, but a sudden fit of laughter rippled through her. Even as she lay there with the rain pelting down on her, the sky darkened even more. But when that happened, the deluge strangely stopped, and Natalie glanced up, bewildered.

A concerned face under an umbrella appeared over her, shielding her from getting any more wet.

"Are you okay?"

Taking the proffered hand, she rose in embarrassment. The man who helped her to her feet was a nice-looking gentleman with a peppery French beard, strong features and a smile that turned his face boyish. The umbrella made no sense because she was already drenched, but still, he gallantly extended it over her and walked her home.

"Aren't you wet?" she wondered.

"No, I'm Gabe," he returned flippantly, unconcerned that he, too, was quickly getting soaked. He'd been on the street when she slipped in a windmill of arms and went sprawling. But it was her inoffensive laughter at the rain that he found quite appealing. When he reached her gate, he added, "I live at the end of the street."

"I'm Natalie," she smiled, thinking what a strange morning this was turning out to be. "Thank you, Gabe. But won't you come in for some coffee? I was making breakfast when I had an unusual visitor." She broke off and glanced down the road, where the old man had almost vanished.

"I could do with some coffee," Gabe replied, taken in by her smile and hopeful dark eyes. "And maybe a towel, too?"

❧

Obliterated by the sheets of rain, the old man walked down the street. He looked heavenward and wondered what or who was next as he turned onto another block. Perhaps a garishly clad crossdresser?

When the rain cleared, and the street began to dry under the advancing heat, the old man could no more be seen. Instead, dragging a bursting suitcase behind him, a flamboyant youngster with a shock of pink curls and rainbow-coloured pants fluttered down the street, looking for a place to stay.

VII
Finding Marina

In the light before dawn, Greg and Pete detected the cabin across the valley, snug in a hollow of undergrowth. A glow of light filtered dully from one window in front, but otherwise, all was silent.

Both men were quiet. Except for the deep gasps of one man unconditioned to the outdoor life and the measured footsteps of his partner, who was, there were no other sounds.

Even the pre-dawn bird calls seemed to have vanished into a void.

The hollow was a hewn-out face in the rock, high on a slope where trees clung precariously. Like an open mouth on a fully bearded face, it was thickly concealed with eucalyptus trees and dense undergrowth. Yet, the clearing itself, where the cabin stood, appeared bare.

Dawn was breaking when they descended into the valley and began to trudge upslope towards the hollow. Greg heard his partner's laboured gasps and slowed down. He turned and waited for Pete.

"You know," the individual panted. "She's always going to remember the kind of man you are."

"And what kind would that be, Pete?" Greg's voice was deep, tired, and edgy. He longed for a quick nap—ten—five minutes—anything. They had been on the road and in the forests for two days straight with very little food and no rest. Both were exhausted and about ready to murder each other. Pete's comment about his future wife irritated Greg.

"Well," and Pete shrugged. He was a prosecution lawyer skilled in dialogue – especially the kind that slashed and marred his victims. "Remind me again how many women you've been with?"

The anger welling deep inside Greg didn't surface. The only indication of it was a raised eyebrow on a hard face. The tense two days and nights were beginning to show. He looked like a lean, hungry man of the mountains, with a white shirt unbuttoned to his broad, muscular chest and khaki trousers about his lean hips. He didn't allow his anger to get the better of him. His eyes shed the fury and sparkled with intelligence, goodwill, and patience. Folks who didn't know Greg Jefferson too well were always taken aback that he was a professor of Economics at the local college in his hometown. He smiled at Pete Mitchell, and his face turned boyish.

"It's a record. You wouldn't even get close to breaking it."

"I happen to have been raised right," came the self-righteous but outrageous response. "But do you think Marina can live with that?"

"It's pretty obvious she doesn't want to!" Greg laughed, and Pete, realising that he had cornered himself into a verbal trap, grinned too. He was a step downslope and wheezing and knew that if Greg swung his leg out, he'd plummet. Still, in some weird way, he compared his rival to a gnawing toothache. He wanted to prod it, dig it, to see how far the pain would go.

"Marina always said that the most perfect love is a first love," he added. "So, while you'll be her first, do you think she'll like bringing up the rear?"

"Why don't you ask her, Pete?" Greg, all banter vanishing, suggested in a low voice. He knew all too well that the man glancing up at him with dislike – respect perhaps but arch dislike – was insane over his fiancé.

There was history here. Last month, Marina had called off her engagement with Pete Mitchell; she didn't love him. She had always loved Greg. Saying yes to Pete had been a terrible rebound after she and Greg had broken up the year before.

They had now got back together again and had planned on getting married. But the day before yesterday, all hell had broken loose. Marina had vanished in the middle of making breakfast. Her mother had called Greg in total panic when the kitchen began to fume with smoke, and Marina could not be found. Uzziah, a young, arrogant and brazen man who had been a habitual in prison and a petty convict, had vanished too, and it didn't take long to put two and two together. The older lady had mentioned that Uzziah had been doing odd jobs around their home, and Marina had appeared agitated and apprehensive.

He was a thief, after all!

"He's taken my girl, Greg," she had wailed. "Kidnapped her for ransom, I'm sure."

When no ransom note came by the end of that day, the police began to follow up on clues. But Greg and Pete, rivals for the same woman's hand, had set out on their own, following through on the knowledge that the petty convict came from a small town at least 200 miles away.

Pete Mitchell loved Marina, and he wished her well. But Greg Jefferson had always been her first love. And Greg loved her too – he wanted to marry and raise children with her. Now, gathering all the clues they could find, the lawyer and the professor had zeroed in on the convict's hometown. A crony who knew the convict had mentioned the cabin, and they now trudged uphill to this place.

Greg's mind was now filled with a million thoughts, shooting blind. Pete was right, wasn't he? Marina was pure, unspoiled, sweet and angelic. He...a rake. He was just another guy who had filled his weekends with a different girl. Wouldn't this always come back to bite him when he and Marina had some argument? Wasn't that a possibility – to be reminded of the time when he had fooled around?

Greg clenched his jaws as he trudged uphill. He loved Marina deeply and wanted to spend the rest of his life with her, but could she spend the rest of her life with him knowing there had been other women?

"She called it off with him, you fool," he admonished himself. "She loves you and wants to marry you."

Behind him, he heard Pete Mitchell's deep breathing.

"I'm sure she loves you, Jefferson," the lawyer said, echoing his thoughts. "But the way I see it, she loves the idea of you—the idea of being married to you—nothing more!"

Greg swung around, working hard to restrain himself. Had it not been for this miserable little man who now taunted him, he would have married Marina back then instead of breaking up with her. He held back. Pete wasn't the one at fault, he realised. They were two men who loved the same woman, that's all.

"Can we focus on the present, Mitchell?" he asked levelly. "Chances are neither of us will ever know what or whom she loves more if we don't find her soon enough."

Pete saw reason and reached upward for Greg's outstretched hand, yanking himself over a small lip in the hill.

"You know, Professor," he began, shaken at the immense strength of the upward pull, "you could have sent me hurtling down this slope."

"What makes you think I didn't want to, Councillor?" Greg retorted with a disarming grin.

"You might need an extra pair of hands in case we got into a fracas there?"

"Or because you aren't worth the effort?"

Pete laughed, and both men slogged upward. Presently, they came to a small overhang under the hollow. Enough vegetation clung to the lip to enable them to hoist themselves up. Even so, the loneliness of the place, the single light from the cabin window and the chilling silence cautioned them. Gingerly reaching upward, Greg pulled himself up on a branch with one arm, had a peek and dropped down again.

"No one seems to be around," he whispered. "Come on."

The hollow was like a stage. The cabin commanded a view all around, except behind. Here, the rock face rose high into the dawning sky. On the far right, a small footpath led down and disappeared into the valley.

"What if Uzziah's around but gone to the back to take a leak?" Pete asked.

"Why would he want to do that?" Greg retorted. "Don't cabins have toilets?"

"Good point!"

"I'm only worried he's carrying a gun," the professor added thoughtfully.

"Uzziah was a petty thief," Pete explained. "Petty thieves don't carry guns."

"Hmm." Greg nodded after giving it some thought. "Let's approach the place from opposite sides."

"Sounds good," agreed Pete. "You approach from the right." He jerked his thumb towards the footpath. "I'll scale up from here."

"Kayo anyone you see."

"Kayo?"

"Knock out. Never done it before? I could show you right now. Small thump?"

"Move it, Professor," Pete grinned, pointing to his right, and Greg hid a smile as he turned.

"She's not gonna go all doe-eyed over you, you know," he said. "Don't you forget I'm the one she wants to marry."

"Only remember it's not going to be perfect for her," Pete taunted in return. "Just because she likes gardening it doesn't mean you're gonna be her rake!"

"Touché!" Greg chuckled and turned to sneak through the brush to the footpath. The light still glowed in the cabin. This had to be the place, Greg thought. It didn't matter who ultimately got to her; he argued with himself as he made it to the path. Whether Marina wanted a rake for her garden or not, she had to be free of this mess.

Trying to heave himself up as Greg had earlier done, Pete's thoughts were not so generous. If he got to Marina and delivered her from this peril, he'd earn brownie points! On his third attempt, he pulled himself up the lip and crouched in the space. The cabin was a yard ahead. He glanced behind him, and the valley dropped into cloudy mist. Across, the dawning sky shimmered like gold. For a moment, he was mesmerised that a worm like Uzziah could own such a place. Then he realised that one could be a thief and still inherit the hard earnings of a dead relative.

He moved towards the window as Greg crouched and ran across from the right. Now, flat against the wall on both sides of the window, the professor put a cautioning finger to his lips. Pete only raised a middle finger back at him.

He edged sideways and peered past the glass, but his jaw turned slack, and his face paled. Ducking, he gestured to Greg to get down on his knees.

"What?" seethed Greg, crouching under the window. "Isn't she in there?"

"Come, let's go," was the only urgent whisper from Pete. With a face drained of blood, he crawled towards the footpath, pulling Greg with him. "Come on!" he hissed. "That's not *our* Marina."

Greg stared incredulously at the retreating figure, and his heart sank. He jerked his hand away. Had they come all this way for nothing? Where was Marina? Wasn't she bound and gagged within this cabin? Why was Pete scurrying away like a mouse? What was in there?

"Don't look, Greg! For God's sake! Don't." Pete frantically beckoned again, but Greg ignored him. He raised himself and peered into the window. For only a second, he appeared bewildered, like a child who had glimpsed something bizarre.

It was a long room, ending in a kitchen worktable. Pots and pans hung above, and an oven was tucked into the wall. The place looked neat. But, as realisation dawned, none of all this mattered. Right before Greg, on the couch beyond the windowpane, was the back of a man's dark tousled head. He, evidently, was having a good time! But looking directly into his flabbergasted face were the lovely brown eyes of the woman he loved.

She was now as startled as he was, but still, her perfect body writhed in a sweaty frenzy, her face wrapped in a combination of astonishment, indignation, embarrassment and... pleasure as she made love to a dashing convict on the couch. Greg Jefferson collapsed to the ground, disgusted.

Pete Mitchell only saw him heave and throw up. With his vision blurring with tears and his throat smarting for his rival, he scrambled on rubbery legs down the footpath, hoping Greg would have the sense to follow him.

VIII

The Yellow Bulbous Buttercup

The early summer sun glinted off the fine hairs glimmering like gold gossamer on Emily's legs.

She didn't appear to care. A sprightly young teen in the dewy spring of her life, she had armed herself with an old encyclopaedia of wildflowers. Now, she picked her way through the shrubs, trying to avoid hurting even the tiniest bloom. The morning dew had moistened her pink shorts, and the springy arm of some hedge had brushed against her arm, leaving a line of tiny, clinging seeds. A smudge of dirt on her knee, resulting from a faulty step and a sprawl, barely bothered her. Emily moved on, intent on her adventures with the flora of the world around her.

A high grey building loomed behind her, where a row of tall, narrow firs appeared to resemble the bars of a prison door. Its massive battlements raking the azure sky were enough proof that it had stood the test of centuries. From within came distant choral voices, echoing sweetly across the meadow and diffusing like fragrance with the benevolent sun. Emily turned once to trace her footsteps back, remotely aware that her presence was needed at that morning practice. Even so, the old encyclopaedia was much more interesting with its many pictures of meadow flowers. Bending, she gently examined a clumpy, deep pink flower in the grass and compared it with a picture in her book.

"Red Clover," she muttered, examining it and ticking off the picture on the page. She moved on, scanning the grass and vigilantly stepping around tiny mauve vetches that appeared commonplace at a glance but were stunning under her magnifying glass.

"How come you're so pretty, and we don't even know?" She winked into the glass and peered at the marvel of nature. Then she gasped in delight and dropped to her knees, feeling a tiny sting where her skin had grazed from her earlier fall. Before her, in the deep green of the moist grass and almost glittering under the dew, was a bunch of little yellow flowers. Their velvet petals formed little cups, shrouding sweet mysteries of pollen deep within. Emily peered at a flower and referred to her book, swiftly turning page after page for the elusive name. She examined the spiky leaves and the thread-like stalk and studied her book, finally seeking a picture that matched it almost completely.

"Bul..bulbous buttercup," she said softly, caressing the yellow texture. "Bulbous..." The awe upon her small, innocent face vanished. Her smile, framed by soft pink lips like fresh rose buds, faded into the whiteness of her pearly white front teeth. A flash of dread mingled with confusion crept into her big, inoffensive brown eyes – not moments earlier, they had been bright with childlike wonder at the beauty in the meadow. The terror dulled to brown pools of reflection, of a secret pang of guilt, and the flower paled even as she stared at it.

Bulbous. That's what the judge had said to the sneering man in the docks:

"You appear to have no remorse," he had said. "Your bearing is arrogant, and your bulbous eyes are derisive. You assaulted a child – the daughter of your lover!"

Emily lay down beside the flower and hugged herself into a tight ball. Two weeks ago, if she had tried to hold herself the way she did now, it would have been uncomfortable with the terrific swelling in her abdomen. Now that was gone. All that remained was the memory of a bewildering struggle, bearing down, and searing pain. Of blood, sweat, tears, and all of that vanishing into physical relief, but greater confusion at a tiny nose, with nostrils so transparent they reminded her of her dolls. But even as that memory came on, red, watery, bulbous eyes overshadowed it, and she hugged herself tighter, shuddering.

The grass now smelled of stale alcohol and sweat and felt like a pelt of hair against her skin. Suddenly, she felt the agony of it all over again. A man had come home – but that hadn't been odd because many men would come – some brought her chocolates, and some brought her ribbons for her hair. They would be kind and caring, like her father, who had gone off to fight a war and had been killed in combat. But this one had crashed in, swearing and drunk, had vanished into a room with her mother, and had raised his voice so loud, she could hear its explosive boom even from behind the closed door. Then he emerged, enraged, turning his lustful attention onto her and ripping her school uniform right off her young, innocent body.

It wasn't hard for the police to find the man – they had picked him up in the local hotel, sleeping off his drink and his act of violence, and had brought him before the magistrate. His reason for his heinous crime upon an innocent young teen had been plain, bland and unremorseful:

"She seemed like a good idea."

But within her own home, Emily's troubles had begun. Her mother, wild with smudged makeup and hair flying like a halo of black fire around her head, only picked up a reed and marked her dazed daughter for the blood that poured down her legs.

"Thirteen and a little whore already," gasped the shattered woman as the reed broke upon Emily's pale, soft skin.

The law sent the man with bulbous eyes to prison for 20 years, but Emily was forced to grow up overnight, to drown in confusion and hang her head in shame. She remembered her struggle two weeks ago, the shadowy women in white shuffling about her and her cries for her mother, who never came. Perhaps she never would come, and in all her childish reflections, Emily tried to understand. She was guilty, too, wasn't she? Otherwise, why would her mother beat her and send her away? Of course, they could not throw her into prison. She was too small and young, so her mother sent her away to a different kind of prison – not the type with bars and high windows, but still, one that closed her in. At least she had the expansive garden full of shrubbery, the grass and the wildflowers. At least she had the old encyclopaedia.

The Bulbous Buttercup shivered in an eddying breeze. Emily watched it and shivered, too. Suddenly, the velvet yellow, concealing deep mysteries of pollen, was distasteful to her. She wanted to run away, across the meadow, over the wall surrounding it, and into the free country beyond, where the blue sky abounded and the green grass was tall and cool.

Back home, her dolls were still in their prams and cradles, staring at the ceiling with marble eyes, fingers frozen in chubby plastic and hair in permanent curls. Her mother would be rising from a bed where, the night before, a strange man had lain with her. Soon, she'd plan on how to occupy herself during the day as she powdered her face and lined her eyes.

Here, Emily was all alone, but for those ladies whose voices still sailed over the meadow to her in heavenly melody. She was all alone except for one doll starting to open its beautiful eyes.

The ladies had thanked God that they were not red and bulbous!

Emily sighed deeply, inhaling the fragrance of the morning. The ladies caring for her were kind-hearted, compassionate, and tender. They were quiet-spoken and given to meditation and prayer. Even their footfalls over the dark, polished flagstone floor of the old castle behind were gentle and soft, as though deeply conscious that a stronger step might awaken the dead in their eternal rest in the walled cemetery on the other side.

She missed her mother in some strange way, like an old man might miss his favourite chair, but the ladies here, dressed in their long white garments, now taught her how to sew, knit, sing and paint. She attended a school in the village and particularly loved her natural science classes. One pretty young teacher had started giving her secret dance lessons, too.

But then, always at the back of her mind and in her sweaty dreams, a big, hairy man with red, watery, bulbous eyes sneered at her and hurt her. Emily jumped up and stared at the yellow bulbous buttercup, the tiny muscle in her jaw moving. Her delicate nostrils flared and turned pink. Her chest heaved, and a soft cry of rage emerged from her throat. The tears came as she raised her foot, her vision blurring. It cleared in a waterfall when she blinked. With a desperate cry, she brought it down hard on the grass. The yellow flower, a hair's breadth from her foot, shuddered from the tiny tremor within the earth. With a deep, long sigh, Emily crashed to her knees again, still hugging her book. A million conflicting thoughts flashed through her young mind, questions with no answers and answers without meaning.

The flower shuddered again as if dreading its surroundings, and Emily's eyes softened. She ran her fingers over the lush green grass, and the coolness brought a sliver of relief. Perhaps, she told herself, if she didn't think of those red, bulging eyes, the grass would smell like grass and not reek like stale alcohol.

Resolutely wiping her tears away, she bent low and examined the bright yellow flower again, blowing gently into its velvet whorls to glimpse the mysteries of its minuscule anthers, style and stigma.

"Bulbous means like a bulb," she vowed under her breath. Then, as she marked a tick on the page, she added, "This is one more flower I can find in my encyclopaedia."

"Emily!"

Over by the enormous grey building and emerging from between the line of thin, tall firs, a senior nun dressed in white with a starched coif sailed out, cradling a tiny baby in her arms.

Emily turned and walked back, reaching forward awkwardly to take her little daughter in her arms.

IX

The Living Dead

"But I saw him bury you."

Carl stared in utter disbelief as Tonya trembled with the terror of the walking dead. It wasn't what she said that stunned him. Nothing surprised him much anymore. After what he had been through, there was little on the planet that could shift the needle of his emotions. But what Tonya said had filled him with amazement.

"Yeah, he did, didn't he?" Carl responded when he finally pulled himself together. "I was lucky," he added with a lopsided grin, turning his features grotesque. "It was a shallow grave, so it wasn't hard to claw myself out. Did he take all the dough?"

"Y...Yes," she answered, fluttering her terror-struck eyes up at him and quickly averting them. His penetrating gaze was like a shaft of light, delving into the darkest corners of her heart and mind, seeking answers.

Carl, before her in the flesh, was hardly a pleasant sight. His face, scarred from all the brutality of being bashed, beaten, burned and buried alive, told the tale of a terrible adventure. One eye was partially closed with an untidy bulge of skin on an eyelid, torn open and mended by someone hardly proficient in suturing. A knife wound serrated his hard mouth into a crooked sneer, stretching across his cheek to his eye like an angry red centipede. But what horrified her the most were the tiny clumps of burn scars, like small waves upon a fleshy ocean. It ravaged the other side of his face and melted his ear into a lump of flesh.

Carl had been such a good-looking man! And they had been a couple, too.

"He took every penny," she added in a small voice, which he only heard because he had cocked his good ear downwards to catch her words. "And...and he told me if I squealed, then he'd squeal too, and we'd both end up in the slammer. So, he set me up in this place ...." Both pairs of eyes swept over the adequately furnished bungalow room. "He's been giving me an allowance to get by," she added.

Carl laughed; it was a weird, ugly laugh. He sat beside her and clasped her hand. His eyes, the only aspect of his features that remained unchanged, turned almost soft and pitying.

"Well," he said. "He's now in a place where he can never harm you, Tonya."

She snapped her head around to him. It was horrible to look upon his face at such close quarters, but what he said filled her with greater dread.

"What do you mean?" she asked breathlessly.

"I mean just that." His smile was a grimace. "After we cleaned that bank out and after our scrap, he buried me thinking I was dead. Well," Carl shrugged. "When I came around – it wasn't hard to get out of the pit he'd flung me into – I spent six months nursing myself back to health and kept a low profile in one of those towns along the highway. They don't have the best doctor." He made a circular gesture around his face to drive home his point. "Then," he added as his eyes hardened, "I tracked him down."

Tonya trembled.

"You did?"

He stood up to examine a figurine of Themis on the piano and gently tapped the tiny brass scales.

"Yes," he replied and turned towards her, smiling with grotesque ease. "I found him last week and took him back to where he'd buried me." He looked at his hands; she did too, and for the first time, Tonya noticed the burn-scarred fingers and half-grown nails. Most likely, he'd lost some of them in his frantic effort to dig himself out from the grave. She imagined the battle and nearly gasped for air herself.

"I took him back," Carl said, sitting beside her again. "Then I buried him in that very hole. Only this time, he was dead, and that grave was a lot deeper."

Tonya sat still, her hands clasped tight in her lap. A tear rolled down her cheek as she shuddered at the memory.

"Remember, after we got away, we stopped on the highway to remove our masks?" she asked.

"He slugged me from behind?"

She nodded.

"Then he flung you into the trunk," she explained. "When I tried to fight him, he knocked me out too and tied me up in the back seat. I remember we were driving through the night when I came around, and I don't know where we stopped. Then he dragged you out of the car and took you somewhere. It was too dark ...."

"I know," Carl said, touching her shoulder. Tonya cringed and felt a shudder almost split her spine apart. It was as if a dead man had touched her. "I'd almost come around by then, but my head was bleeding, and I was nauseated. I remember calling out to you, but he was already beating me up and pouring gasoline over me. The last thing I remember was fighting the fire. I called out and called out to you for help," he added, shaking his head.

"Carl, I couldn't," she whimpered. "He bound me in the car, and I couldn't move, and I had no clue what he'd done to you. All I know is he returned without you. I've been living in fear of him ever since and doing his every bidding. I'm so glad you're okay, darling."

Tonya struggled to smile.

"I called out for you," he said again with regret.

"I wish I'd known what he had done and where he had buried you," she whispered, trying to touch the disfigured hands. "Did you find the money, Carl?" she asked with an expectant glance at his awful face.

"I did," he replied indifferently. "But Tonya, it doesn't sound right, does it?" He looked straight at her, and his eyes were now expressionless. "I mean, you just said you saw him bury me!"

Tonya froze, and her mouth went dry. Then she closed her eyes and hoped he'd be quick.

X

Back to Square One

Dr Simon Halliday guzzled from a bottle and escaped to his apartment.

Over the thin wall between his and his neighbour's flats, he heard whimpers and cries for help. He flopped to the carpet and rolled over on his back, staring at the ceiling. A tear fell down the side of his face and tickled into his ear.

He suppressed a tremor in his hands and admonished himself. How long had it been? Three months? How different was it now from three months ago? In truth, not much. It was all the same, and he was back to square one.

He advised himself that before the police arrived, it would be good to retrospect. He was going to do just that...with a bottle of cheap whiskey firing his mind and flowery curtains blooming in his window.

The curtains were black three months ago, and his flat was a garbage dump! That night, when he had crashed to the floor drunk, breaking a bottle, he had heard a yell! Over the thin wall, he listened to his neighbours fight. He knew he'd soon hear a door bang, and Bart would go to his mother's house for a week.

As he had predicted, a door slammed, and he heard Charlie weeping. He knew she would cry for a day and then start picking up the pieces of her dignity. She'd go out, return, smile at him, and things would be the same as before the time that narcissist had moved in. He'd hear her cleaning, smell her cooking, and sometimes listen to her singing in the evening.

Simon secretly loved Charlie and was shattered when Bart had shacked up with her. Gosh! If he only had a little courage, maybe both their flats could have become one. His last thought that night was an image of her cheerful face as he drifted into a drunken stupor. He must have crawled onto the couch at some time in his sleep because he was deep in it when he woke the following day. He sniffed hash browns and bacon frying and told himself that dreaming of food was the last thing he needed after a hard night of drinking.

He sat up, his mind reeling with confusion!

The mess in the room after two weeks of binge drinking was gone! Bottles, empty cigarette packs, stale takeaway food, soiled napkins, dirty laundry – all were gone. To convince himself he was not dreaming, he glanced at the floor to locate the broken bottle pieces. That, too, had vanished!

Was he in his parents' house? The Full English breakfast wafting from the kitchen suggested it. But a hard ashtray under his buttocks negated the idea. He shifted, pulled it free, and rubbed his rear to regain circulation. The washing machine banging away told his foggy brain that a wash cycle was on. The carpet looked vacuumed by his feet, and the other couches appeared tidied. The cushion covers were missing, though! The curtains, too, and he wondered what sort of thief would clean his home, cook his breakfast, and swipe his furnishings.

The answer came a moment later when a girl entered, armed with a ladle.

"Simon," she smiled, and he gaped at her.

Charlie, his next-door neighbour! The girl he secretly loved!

Her eyes were swollen from all the crying, but she smiled brightly. Simon's breath caught. Slack-jawed, he could only stare.

"You're up," she observed cheerfully. "Good. Come, I've made us breakfast."

Despite his astonishment, Simon groaned nauseously at the idea of food and made a beeline to the toilet.

When he regained control of his stomach and rinsed his mouth, he gasped at the cleanliness of everything. What had Charlie done? Disinfected his home? Taken his bachelor's establishment and thrown it into the garbage?

After he had been suspended from the hospital two weeks earlier due to aggressive behaviour while on duty, Dr Simon Halliday had hit the bottle. The great Doc Halliday, he called himself when in a sarcastic and self-flagellating mood. The only thing was that the real Doc Holliday was a 'lunger' and a gunfighter. The fake Doc Halliday was a loser and a boozer!

When he gingerly peered into the room, he found breakfast on the table and Charlie covering the cushions with clean covers.

"Um," Simon cleared his throat. "Charlie? You here?"

Her face clouded, and she slumped forward with the cushion on her lap.

"Please don't tell him I'm here, Simon," she begged. "We fought last night!"

"Yeah – I heard," he replied. "Do you think it's wise? I mean, you being here?"

"I've nowhere else to go."

She hugged the cushion, and her eyelids fluttered down. When she turned her face up again, Simon noticed her eyes brimming with tears. "Please let me stay for a couple of days—a week at most."

"But..." Simon wanted to tell her that Bart should have been the one to leave. Not her. It was *her* flat.

"I know. I know what you're thinking," Charlie said but guessed incorrectly. "I'll sleep on the couch and keep very quiet. Only a few days. Please."

Simon scratched his head. He was still flummoxed and suffering a rollicking hangover. "How did you get in?"

"The door was open."

It was as simple as that.

He left the room quickly and in confusion. Why would she choose his home for shelter? As neighbours, he barely spoke to Bart. They were two different men. Bart was a trainer at the local gym – muscled and trim. Simon Halliday was a debarred emergency doctor!

One week, he told himself. In hindsight now, he wished he had moved back with his parents. It would have been the best course to take instead of staying on at his flat and ruining his life again.

By the evening of that day, Simon recalled, both were giggling like children, hiding behind his front door and listening to Bart's movements in and out of the next apartment. He stoutly decided to keep away from the bottle that day. Anyway, he told himself, to drink, he'd have to replenish his supply, and for that, he'd need to leave his flat. He wasn't sure how he'd react if he met Bart. Bart would ask him about Charlie, and Simon didn't want to lie.

"Which one," Charlie asked him the next day, holding up two sets of curtains. "This one with the tiny flowers I found in the drawer, or this black one which is now washed and free of all food grime?"

Laughing at Simon's gaping and confused face, she added, "Yes. You were using it to wipe food off your hands! That is absolutely disgusting!"

"Not the flowers, please," he answered and grinned sheepishly. "That's what my mum gave me."

"Well, she has taste," came the immediate response. "The flowers are pretty and will brighten this room."

Charlie was right, and Simon couldn't believe how cosy the room had become. The soft light from the window made everything feel sunny and warm.

On the following day, they heard Bart speaking loudly on the phone. He paced the common area between their flats and sounded angry. Behind the door, Simon and Charlie crouched, listening intently. He couldn't help but notice her pink cheeks and shining eyes and was amazed at the redness in her lips. Nothing, he realised, nothing suggested that she was a runaway girlfriend!

"What do you find in him?" he whispered tactlessly. "To me, he's only a narcissistic jerk!"

Charlie giggled, and Simon detected mischief in her shining eyes. "You're enjoying this, aren't you?" he mouthed. "He's calling all your friends asking if you're with them."

"Hush! Listen...."

Outside, Bart, unsuccessful with the calls he'd been making, howled in rage. They heard the phone shatter and quick footsteps shuffle across the floor. Then, a door slammed shut.

Charlie bit her finger and giggled again, a soft little laugh that sounded like a music note. On an impulse, Simon reached forward and kissed her. It took her completely off guard, and she stared at him for a moment. The next second, she flew into his lap and kissed him back.

That night, Charlie moved from his couch to his bed, and the week stretched to a month, and a month stretched to two. She and Bart broke up after a stormy showdown one day, and he moved out – likely to his mother's house.

With their two flats side by side, the new lovers began looking at designs to combine their homes. Simon could not have been more satisfied. All he needed to do now was clear his name at the hospital.

"So, why were you suspended?" she asked him one night.

"Long story," he replied. "I'm under what you call suspension, pending enquiry."

"But why?"

"I hit a patient's dad who tried to tell me how to do my job."

She stared, flabbergasted, at him.

"The kid had overdosed and was having seizures," he went on to explain. "And the dad was dancing around telling me what to do. So, I decked him."

She giggled. "That's so unlike you, Simon Halliday."

"Oh! I'm a superhero in scrubs," he joked and pounced on her, pinning her to the bed.

At that moment, they heard a crash outside the flat. Glancing at each other bewildered, they tumbled out of bed and charged to the front door. Opening it, Simon gasped aloud. Charlie, behind him, let out a tiny scream.

Sliding down the door of her flat, Bart was bloody and beaten, his nose a mass of pulp. Simon was already by his side, checking his pulse and examining his broken nose. When he tried to lift him, the big man winced. A quick inspection of his abdomen confirmed his fears, and Simon gritted:

"Charlie, he has a few broken ribs. Call the cops. Call an ambulance."

"No, no," Bart's voice was raspy and his breath was shallow. "No cops. No hospital. They're after me."

"Who?"

"Some jerks from the gym!"

"You're a fool to come here!" Simon admonished. "Charlie, help me get him to a bed."

She had been standing like a mass of granite by Simon's door. Flying into action at his order, she ducked under Bart's heavy arm and supported him as they helped him into her flat. Laying him on the bed, Simon immediately turned to Charlie and asked her to bring him warm water and clean sheets.

Taking care of Bart in the next flat was easy. For one, being a doctor, Simon knew what to do. Secondly, the stricken man had the most attentive nurse in Charlie. Within a week, Bart was able to speak, and in a month, he was already shuffling about the apartment. Charlie was his constant nurse, most so because Simon's enquiry into his conduct at the hospital had commenced. It was likely that he would be let off with only a warning. For Simon, it had been a week of running around, retrieving camera footage, finding witnesses and getting his rebuttals together. But in the end, he was back to being Dr Simon Halliday again.

Jubilant, he came home with a bottle of whiskey to give Charlie the news. Aware that, with her patient needing attention, she wouldn't be in his apartment, he charged into hers and into the room of convalescence. But then, at the door, he froze as if something had slapped his face. Bart might have been recovering from two broken ribs, but both his hands now were working double time as he fondled his giggling nurse and rolled on top of her.

Something exploded inside Simon, and he roared in fury. Charging wildly, he pounced on the injured man, yanked him off the screaming girl and punched him repeatedly in the ribs. When he had reduced Bart to whimpers of agony, Dr Halliday bunched his fist and walloped the tender nose, feeling the delicate cartilage crumple under his knuckles.

As Bart writhed in suffering and Charlie screamed in terror, Simon retrieved his bottle and left the flat.

Cheap whisky, but it would do.

XI
Froth

Dolly lay crumpled on her bed.

Like a papery corpse, she lay, bones jutting where, at one time, pink flesh might have fired a young man's dreams. The only thing was, the 'young man,' Eddie, had died a day before his 82nd birthday, battling total paralysis of his physical body.

Her middle-aged sons tried to whisper the sad news to her. They had only just buried their father and were raw - not from their bereavement, but from the cruel reality that their mother might never comprehend that she was now a widow. And perhaps Dolly didn't.

Her lucid moments were but fleeting. Sometimes, she'd hear a doctor whisper big words - akinetic Parkinson's Disease or complete muscle atrophy or even advanced Alzheimer's, and her mind would blip with some cognition - a passing memory of her mother who died of something similar. Still, like a rapidly advancing frothy cloud, her mind would become eclipsed. Experiences would be lost! Nothing remained but some notion of existence, of feathery memories floating aimlessly on the black ocean of her mind.

Nurses would bathe her every day, carry her rigid body and crumple it into a wheelchair to give her a little sun. Dolly would slump into her shoulder and stare at nothing because it didn't make sense anymore. Yes, she had thoughts. They beeped through her mind but were like jumbled words that connected nowhere and made no sentences. She heard people talk - sometimes a word brought back a memory, but in seconds, it was swallowed, like a drop of colour churning in a tub of white cream to lose its essence in the thick, snowy vortex of foam!

That day, she lay in her bed, cardboard straight and staring when her two sons visited.

"Mum," said one, drawing close to her ear. "Mum, Daddy's no more. Eddie's no more."

Her gaze at some unseen spot on the hospice ward ceiling never faltered. What was Mum? What was Daddy? What was no more? What was Eddie? They were only words hanging from silken threads. Words unconnected, unrelated, with no beginning, no end. What was beginning? What was end? What was *what*?

Her son glanced at his older brother and shook his head. The other only shrugged. Dolly stared at the ceiling, ignoring or oblivious to the shifting blobs beside her bed. She felt something warm touch her...her son had bent down and kissed her forehead. Something warm touched her again - her other son had done the same, but in the froth of her mind, the warmth was quickly swallowed, like essence disappearing in a whirlpool of clouds.

Long after the blobs had left her, she still stared at the unseen spot on the ceiling. Her brow twitched where a fly frolicked, and for a fleeting moment, she recognised the irritant. She tried to slap her head, to kill the fly in its mischief, but the atrophy in her limbs had turned her rigid. If Dolly felt a pang of dread that she had lost all movement, it was whisked away into the ocean of darkness where water churned, but no ships of reason sailed. Still, later that night, when the nurse came to change her and to feed her nasally, Dolly was taken up by the lovely pink of the girl's uniform. It was so pleasing to the eye! She tried to say it, but the atrophy had frozen her jaws, too, and every voluntary muscle in her body. If Dolly weren't breathing, she would have only been a piece of living blockboard!

The pink blipped across her mind, out and into the froth. The blob shifted around her, moved her, lifted her, settled her and left her.

Deep in the night, a fleeting memory of a whisper in her ear returned:

"Mum, Daddy's no more. Eddie's no more."

Dolly swallowed hard, feeling the harsh food tube deep in her throat. Her eyes prickled and filled painfully as she ground her teeth. Of course, she remembered Eddie at that moment. He was like a little lifeboat bobbing on that mighty black ocean where froth, like the lace of her wedding gown, bubbled on the waves. He was the love of her life. She had given him sons, and they had been proud parents. They had been married fifty-five years, and what a life it had been! They had loved, fought, broken up, made up and loved again. They had run the rat race of life, sighed in fatigue at a long day's end, and rose again the following day to fight new battles. Some they won, many they lost, but still they had held on to each other, even in those darkest times when every light had winked and died, but for one, their intense love and devotion to each other.

And then, in the twilight of their years, when couples dream of sitting on their back porch watching the sunset and calling their grandchildren from their play, Eddie had a stroke which paralysed his whole body. She remembered him in his bed, twisted and mute, a tongue so thick, he couldn't say her name! That's all she remembered.

Where was she now, she wondered. Maybe in the next room? When had Eddie died? Why was she here in bed, unable to move when she needed to be kissing his face for the last time? She tried to move, to shout, to cry, but no sound came. Only her throat burned more and brought up a cough. A nurse ran to her aid, raised her head and quietened the spasm.

In all of this, perhaps Dolly's bottom lip became caught in the gnashing and grieving because, in the morning, the nurses found her with her mouth swollen and bleeding.

They wondered aloud what might have happened and asked her, knowing they would not get an answer.

Dolly only stared at her window. The clouds were like froth outside, but she would never comprehend.

XII
Eve's Reflection

When God created Eve, He made her perfect! Perfect in beauty, stature, strength, disposition, intelligence, fertility, resilience, and love. She was, after all, His last project in the whole design of creation, and with her powerful XX chromosome, He made her flawless! Yet God, in His omniscience, also knew that such an impressive creature was capable of excessive control. With her superlative abilities, she would dominate, and from 'impressive,' she could transform into 'redoubtable!'

He didn't want that, obviously. He wanted Eve to walk hand in hand with Adam, her mate – she was made from his side. God wanted her to remain by his side – not above him.

So, he planted a little germ in her head.

Doubt.

Thus, we are not one bit surprised at the age-old 'Dad Joke', passed down through the ages, which runs:

"Adam, do you love me?"

"Woman, who else is there?"

It doesn't end there, and God chuckled from his heavenly seat. Down in the Garden, Adam woke to find Eve counting and, doubtfully, re-counting his ribs!

Fast forward generations later, Eve, from her station in Heaven, gazed down upon a lovely creature perfect in every aspect, except the one, and shook her head in exasperation at her Creator.

Frances, our twenty-something heroine of today, indeed, was fleeing into that realm of doubt. Sighing before her looking glass, she applied the finishing touches to her makeup and examined her face.

She was a lovely girl, dark-haired with glossy curls, a button nose, and almond eyes – brown and sparkling. Her lips were full and heart-shaped, and her chin was visually pleasing – not arrogant or docile either. Her complexion was pink and flawless. There wasn't a freckle or tiniest scar to mar it, and when she smiled, the soft creases on her skin turned many breathless.

Frances was lovely!

Still, she peered with a critical eye into the mirror. It was one look repeated at least a hundred times that afternoon. This last look was only meant to be a passing glance, but when something caught her attention, she peered harder. A shudder of awkwardness enveloped her. With a sinking heart, she realised that her lovely, smooth and youthful face had one flaw! And it was a serious defect!

One of her beautiful brown eyes was smaller than the other!

She couldn't believe it. She had never noticed the offending eye in all her days of preening, combing, and beautifying! They were asymmetrical, and she squirmed! But more than that, what would her love, Greg, think of them?

She rubbed the offending sense organ and examined herself once more. It remained unchanged. With a pang, she realised this was how she had always looked! Only she hadn't noticed! With a bigger pang, she realised that this was likely how Greg had seen her, with one eye smaller than its twin! On an impulse, she simpered at her reflection, and her crinkling eyes redeemed her face, but how could one keep smiling forever? Frances groaned and looked away. She wanted to look flawless, immaculate, and symmetrical for Greg!

Resolving not to look at herself again, she settled her dress and added the final touches to her makeup. But for that, she needed the mirror again! Then, suddenly, a thought struck her as she patted her hair, carefully avoiding looking at her face. Thinking made her bite her pretty lips and knit her brows.

"Silly you," she admonished herself. "You're dressed on the chance he'd turn up. And even if he does turn up with you dressed for Sunday Church, he's likely to think you're going out and will leave in a snap."

And she flicked her fingers to drive the point home.

The thought was sobering, resulting in cotton and cleanser wiping off the makeup. She undressed, slipping into a well-pressed T-shirt that accentuated her bosom and figure-hugging jeans. The denim would hurt around her waist, especially when she sat, but she swore she could manage. A second after the wiggling, the buttoning, and the zipping up, Frances found herself in a fashion dilemma again!

She, indeed, was uncomfortable!

Once more, her intelligence kicked in. If she retained the T-shirt but slipped into her shorts, she'd have a moment to jump into her jeans if and when the doorbell rang! That was an idea. So, with a dance of her hips, the jeans came off, and the shorts went on. Frances felt better – freer.

She sat down to read, but that activity was frequently interrupted by expectant gazes at the clock and impatient listening for a footstep at her door. Sighing loudly, she chucked the book aside and wondered about her eyes again. Would they look better now?

For the hundred-and-first time that afternoon, Francis approached her ever-truthful reflection and found, to her dismay, that there was no change at all. Her eyes still appeared unequal. She moaned and stomped her foot, and the mirror did the same back to her.

"I hate you," she told her reflection, and the mirror echoed silently.

What if, she wondered, she drew attention away from her eyes by styling her hair in a topknot? A YouTube tutorial promised instructions for an effortless coiffure, and she promptly started the video on her phone.

But it was easier said than done, for it was a battle with brush, pins, and rubber bands! With determination dancing on her face, which made her prettier, if only she could believe her reflection, she told herself that since she was waiting for Greg, she might as well do something to pass the time. So, Frances persisted with her hairdo.

Now, there was a hitch with the adorable Greg's visit.

Frances had no idea if he would drop in in the first place! When he had taken her as his partner for the Yuletide Ball last Christmas, she had fallen in love with him. A perfect descendant of Adam, Greg was such a handsome young man, tall, strong and confident. Now, it was nearing Valentine's Day, and she had learnt from a common friend that he was in town on a short holiday to visit his mother. Starry-eyed from the Christmas Dance, the only notion she wanted to harbour was that he was in town to see his mother *and* visit her.

The arm-breaking hair ritual was soon over, but like all YouTube tutorials, what one saw onscreen versus the outcome was like chalk and cheese! Frances realised she looked ridiculous! First, the hairstyle did not suit the texture of her hair. She had curly locks – the woman in the video had lovely, straight tresses, allowing careless wisps to trail down the side of her face. Secondly, Frances had a wider brow – glancing critically at it now, she realised she hated her forehead too! What would Greg think?

The pins came loose, and the rubber bands tore hair strands from their roots, resulting in a halo of unruly curls.

"Aaah!" she cried in frustration, scattering her hairstyling tools. Calming down quickly with the sobering thought that she was being immature, Frances puffed, reached for a simple bungee, and tied up her hair.

The doorbell rang at that moment, and her heart almost dropped to her knees.

"Coming," she yelled, dancing with her shorts at her ankles and squirming into her jeans.

Dressed again, she settled her T-shirt, poked her bosom out and charged to the door.

Her face, pink with a broad welcoming smile to negate the effect of the asymmetrical eye, clouded. Her younger brother, Paulie, buried in his phone, shouldered past her and disappeared inside.

Frances stared at him as the warm, fuzzy feeling of a rewarding wait ended in the cramping of her thighs. The yard and the street in front were empty and silent under the afternoon sun. A distant engine of a car raised her expectations for only a second, but as the metallic roar faded, so did her hopes. Frances strolled to the street to look up, down and up again. There was no sign of Greg. She sighed, slumped her shoulders and returned indoors.

Frances now felt like a heart-shaped balloon fizzing out. Only she wasn't shooting around the room like an ebullient rubber missile.

It was her asymmetrical eye, she vowed. It had to be.

Greg had enjoyed himself at the Christmas dance and even tried kissing her. Sadly, at that very instant, she had been distracted by another girl who had whooped at the band! With a groan, she now whined softly that she had exposed her smaller eye to his direct view! A blush burned on her cheeks. Another beeline to the mirror confirmed her worst fears all over again.

"No! No! No!" came a wail that sailed heavenward and into Eve's lap. "Why me, God? Why me?"

"What do you mean why you?" she heard Paulie ask, and she felt his quizzical gaze on her.

Frances averted her eyes and looked at his reflection—his perfect, boyish face, dark eyelashes, and tilted eyebrow. Even his eyes appeared perfect, she realised. Then she looked again, noted an asymmetrical feature identical to hers, and swung around to face him, astonished. Weirdly, on a direct glance, nothing appeared uneven! His face still seemed perfect!

"What?" he asked, flabbergasted at her slack jaws. "Are you nuts?"

"Don't move!" she ordered, averting her eyes to his reflection again. Sure enough, the eyes appeared somewhat lopsided, but they were now glimmering, annoyed at her.

"You are nuts!" he confirmed and left the house.

Frances frowned at him, cast a disheartened glance at her reflection and vanished into her room to sulk.

Of course, that was why Greg didn't come...or call, she dejectedly told herself, wistfully glancing at her phone. Swiping to his name and number, she debated about calling him. A long stare at his name only made the waiting more painful. She clumped into a ball on her bed and felt the waistline of her jeans dig into her midriff – but that didn't hurt as much as the notion that she wasn't good enough. Casting her phone aside, she undressed, donned the shorts again with an old but comfortable T-shirt and meandered back to the couch to watch a movie. The flick must have been boring because when her brother returned, chatting over his shoulder to another tall figure who followed, he found the front door open, and his sister leaned back, snoring softly with a dribble on her chin.

"Well, look who's on a siesta," he grinned.

The other chuckled, sat down beside her and pulled out a handkerchief.

Paulie, however, intent on mischief, was faster. Rushing forward, he brought his hands together in a resounding clap before his sister's face and shook with strident laughter.

"Hey! Don't do that!" the other admonished, but Frances had already started awake to the gentle touch of fabric on her chin and a handsome face hovering over her own. "Hi there, Sleeping Beauty," he added brightly.

"Greg?" she murmured. Then realisation set in, and she sat up, mortified. She had asymmetrical eyes, was dressed in an old T-shirt, and dribbled like a baby when she slept! Still, Greg sat close, smiling warmly, and his intense gaze was filled with complete awe and admiration.

"Does he have a problem with his eyes too?" wondered Frances, blushing and fighting to hide a hole in her T-shirt.

"I'm sorry he woke you up like that," Greg whispered. "I wanted to, but with a kiss."

Paulie rolled his eyes and left the room.

Watching from above, Eve breathed in her husband's ear, "Do you love me, Adam?"

"You silly woman, who else is there?"

"Well, there's Frances."

"And there's Greg," he grunted, pointing to the couple cuddling on the couch. "Now, for His sake, don't start counting my ribs!"

God chuckled at the couple.

XIII

Good Riddance To Bad Rubbish

Marjorie Wilson was a battered wife.

Battered, but not beaten.

She was a frail young woman, married eight years and a survivor of three miscarriages, all in the last five years. The pregnancies might have blossomed into bouncing children, but her husband, Patrick, preferred to bounce her around their home when the fancy caught him. It started as playful pushes, which escalated to more serious shoves and finally to extreme physical and sexual abuse. Then, when he found he liked hearing her soft pleas for mercy, it pleasured him to double the whipping, leaving her a pathetic clump of tears and bruises. He was a disgruntled, self-employed, travelling salesman of refrigeration equipment, the type used by big food and meat companies. Brow-beaten by demanding clients, Patrick, 40, was the type of creature who blamed his vulnerability on his wife. It was a twisted form of revenge on the people he hated, and because he couldn't beat them up, he took out his frustrations on her. He was 12 years her senior, had no known family and had a strange habit of collecting knives, axes and choppers. He had an array of them, all displayed along their living room walls, like the barbaric armoury of some Viking Lord. Folks around feared for Marjorie when Patrick Charles Wilson wasn't on his travels. They also wondered what she found in him. True, he was a handsome man. But he was also a psychopath, a charmer before marriage, but a beast in the years that followed.

Marjorie wasn't always fragile. She was quite a pretty lady with intelligent eyes and a smile that could brighten the darkest day. Well-educated, she might have found a job as a technician in a Forensic Science lab, but her tyrannical husband would have none of it. He believed in male supremacy. He stated that a wife's place was at home and beat her into believing it. Marjorie, being of unassuming disposition, or at least exhibiting this side of her character to him, assented to his demands. With meek subjugation, she pushed herself right down in her list of priorities, placing Patrick and her obedience to him at the top. Still, her interests were unwavering, and Marjorie spent her free time absorbed in the literature of police investigation files and videos.

The one hope she held on to, which she often whispered to her concerned friends, was that Patrick would change one day. When they married, he had been a good man – life had turned him into a monster. Her patience could change him back. Dark-haired and diminutive, there was a spark in her eyes that no amount of beating could douse and a quiet smile that veiled her thoughts. Her mother, Miranda Curtis, doted on her and wished she could free her child from such a disastrous union. But then, her daughter wasn't giving up, and neither was Patrick going to *give* her up!

Marjorie was also the pride and joy of her neighbourhood. Her friends loved her. Even a smart young police officer, Mike Harding, had an eye for her but not the courage to tell her. It was reasonable. She had a fiend for a husband who needed no reason to beat her within the confines of their home – for outside, he was like a saint!

The neighbourhood knew of Marjorie's plight and came forward to help. But the doe-like creature, long-suffering and patient, deterred them from taking action. Patrick, she explained, was a wounded man. His scars were taking time to heal, and she was ever hopeful they would. The neighbours went away shaking their heads at the sweetness and tolerance of a wife who had seen little love and honour from the man who had promised it to her. Mike Harding had been most disheartened at her stout refusal to complain formally about the brutality. Being a police officer, her endurance and his impotence, as a result, annoyed him.

She did have companionship, though – her two young dogs. Massive, bulky crossbreeds, the brother-canines were the offspring of a rottweiler father and a mongrel mother. The resultant pups had the sweet innocence of a 'mutt' face but the bulk of a monster, and Marjorie doted on them. Patrick tolerated them to the extent that he would brandish his knives before them in a wild display of swordsmanship only to incite them to snarling and barking.

"You'd relish me, wouldn't you? You sons of bitches," he'd taunt. "What would you not give to have some of me for your dinner?" And much to poor Marjorie's horror, he'd laugh and promise he'd have their heads someday.

She cooked their food twice daily, in the morning and the evening. It consisted of chicken, beef, or mutton cut into chunks, rice, vegetables, and a dash of turmeric—because it was good for their fur and overall health—blended with the meat—and the dogs wolfed it down. She'd stock up their food every week in a big fridge in the outhouse, where she maintained their own kitchen and was content to cook for them.

One evening, Marjorie bent her energies to this chore as her mother critically watched her. Then, with a shake of her head, the older woman left the outhouse.

"I hope I'll be able to say, '*good riddance to bad rubbish*' tomorrow," were her callous, parting words, and Marjorie sighed.

She closed the pot of meat and vegetables and slid down the wall to breathe deeply in some weird combination of sorrow, joy, relief and expectation. One of Patrick's blades was beside a table in the corner; she mentally told herself this wasn't the place for it. Still, Marjorie didn't move. Hugging herself, she only wanted to explore why she was sorry, resist the explosion of joy and breathe in relief.

Tomorrow would be a long day, but she had to steel herself for it.

Then, the past three months came hurtling back, and Marjorie went over everything in her mind again, wondering if she had gone wrong anywhere.

Three months ago, Patrick, with unprovoked rage, had sent her crashing to the floor. He was travelling early the following morning to West Waterfront, a seaside town in the neighbouring county, and his wife had started packing his suitcase a little late which had nettled him. Rising from her disgrace, Marjorie resumed her task, but Patrick, incensed that she didn't so much as even whimper, locked the door, picked up his belt and lashed her with it. The dogs howled outside the room and pawed at the door. Marjorie only resigned herself to her husband's viciousness.

When she took all his violence, he, enraged by her resilience, ripped off her clothes and pounced on her like a beast encountering its female kind for the first time in its existence.

"I'm going to pound you so bad," he howled. "You lazy, lazy slut!"

When he was done, Marjorie only rose, trembled back into her clothes and numbly opened the door to the crazed dogs.

They bounded in, each flying on top of her and then on him, smothering both with elation and love. Tumbling to the floor again, Marjorie only saw, through her vision blurred with tears, that a dog was over her husband, rolling a great tongue over his face and whining with excitement. Then the creature yelped as a fist crashed into its side. It skittered away from the brutal man and regarded him with big, confused brown eyes. Marjorie shuddered in a spasm of rage. It was one thing to batter her. Punching a poor, affectionate mutt was quite something else!

By the following morning, all was silent again – as it always was when Patrick went away on his trips.

Wincing in pain and rising, the battered wife soon realised with a pang of horror that her husband's mobile phone was still charging on the bedside table. Patrick always left some odd thing behind, expecting her to mail it to him at whatever address he was.

Forgetting her bruises, she flew out of bed, snatched up the mobile phone, now fully charged, and found a bubble wrap envelope. In the bathroom, she realised his shaving kit was still in its place.

"Oh no!" she cried, tossing the kit into the envelope along with the phone. "My God! I'll be in trouble if I don't get this to West Waterfront!"

Donning a coat, she ran down the road to the post office and booked the parcel.

"So, he's on his trip again, is he?" said the white-haired post official behind the counter. "And, as usual, forgot some of his stuff?"

He took the package from her pale, white hands and read the address. "He's staying at the Horse and Carriage, eh...West Waterfront? He's now travelling to different counties?"

She nodded again, nibbling a swollen, bruised lip.

"Margie," sighed the old man, coming around the counter as the poor young woman broke down. For some reason, she was high-strung that morning. Perhaps, the post official mused, Patrick had overdone it last night.

"Margie," he said again. "You care so much for that piece of trash. Why are you so sweet to him? If he's forgotten some of his stuff, let him suffer without it for a few days."

"No," she cried vehemently but checked her outburst and added in a softer tone. "He'll only beat me more when he returns."

"How much more are you going to take?"

"He'll change," she insisted with a teary smile. "I know he will."

When Marjorie left the post office, the old official only mentioned on the packet, '*discard if undelivered*', and tossed it into the sorting bag.

Upon returning home, she found her mother waiting for her on the porch, and she rolled her eyes. A big sun hat flopped upon the older woman's head, and bug-like glares shaded her eyes. Miranda Curtis loved to live it up and made the most of it with her only child when Patrick left on his travels. Today would be no exception.

But Marjorie only sighed. She wanted to catch up on sleep after her ordeal the previous night. Sometimes, her mother embarrassed her. Having separated from her own abusive husband years earlier, when Marjorie was a little girl, Miranda loved the free life she lived and wished that her daughter would unwind a little.

"When the cat's away, the mice must play, darling," she'd often say. And true to her sociable character, she now added, "Come, come. I have a packed day for us."

Patrick never called while he was away, and Marjorie never made the mistake of calling him either. The first few times she did, she was subjected to a humiliating beating when he returned. So, even after two weeks, she didn't appear too flustered when there was no sign of her husband. Many times, Patrick would also delay his return. He often would not come home even after three or four weeks, and Marjorie always suspected another woman was the cause. She didn't dare accost Patrick about it, though. For her own safety, she liked to prevent the abuse as much as possible.

When, even after a month, Patrick didn't return or call, Miranda began to worry. Watching her daughter cook up the dogs' food in the shed one morning, she suggested:

"Darling, let's talk to the police. That handsome young policeman...."

Marjorie whirled around, her eyes rolling in anxiety.

"And have Patrick put me up for target practice when he returns? Mother, you know he's done this before."

"Why do you want to live with this trash?" Miranda, steering off-topic, asked hotly. "I took you and left your father. Why don't you do the same?"

"Because I know he'll change."

"It's been eight years, Marjorie! You've lost three babies being slapped around. He doesn't know about two..." Miranda's eyes filled with tears, and her voice broke. "Get out of this marriage before it's too late, my darling. I don't want to be the one burying you."

"You won't," came the soft but firm response, and Marjorie returned to her task.

When six weeks had passed with no sign of the absent wife-beater, a police case was registered. Marjorie, gathering all her courage and laying all misgiving aside, reluctantly placed her complaint before Mike Harding. Numbly, she gave him all the details of Patrick's travel.

"West Waterfront," she said and handed him the hotel address along with his recent photograph. "This is all I have. He rarely told me anything about his work."

Harding took down all details, promised to wire the constabulary of West Waterfront, and warmly escorted Marjorie out, shaking her hand with such affection that she had to pull her fingers free.

"I'll let you know if I hear anything, Margie," he said, wanting to ask her out for coffee sometime. Realising it wasn't appropriate just then, the poor, shy officer held back. Besides, she seemed overcome by anxiety now and didn't look too well.

It was true. Marjorie, at that moment, was fighting a wave of nausea. With a swoon, she crumbled, collapsing into the young man's arms. Being of gallant nature, Mike Harding was only too pleased to carry her inside the station again, sit her down, and massage her palms.

"Relax, sweetheart," whispered the cop, brushing a strand of hair from her face. "I'm here, and I'm going to drive you home."

With the police sending out an 'APB', the case of the truant wife-beater took only two months to solve. Since Patrick had not returned or even tried to contact his wife, the officials concentrated their search for him in the seaside town.

They were quick! When the West Waterfront Police Force found a person who almost fit the description of the missing man, they wired Officer Mike Harding immediately.

Reading the message, Mike whooped in jubilation, and the whole station erupted with loud cheers and whistles. The news was good, and he couldn't wait to meet Marjorie.

"Go tell her, Mikey," they egged him on. "Go tell her and get your girl."

When he and another lady officer called on Marjorie later that afternoon, they had to wait for her on the porch until she returned home.

"I'm sorry," she said when she saw them waiting. Opening her door to her two joyful dogs, she added, blushing, "I had a doctor's appointment."

"All well?" Harding asked, finding himself more and more drawn to her blossoming face. Patrick's disappearance was working wonders on her cheeks, he realised. The tight jeans held up by a man's leather belt with a heavy, fashionable metal buckle gave the impression of a very attractive cowgirl!

Marjorie only smiled; she felt warm, fuzzy and joyful, but intertwined with these beautiful feelings was a vein of anxiousness. Why were the police here?

"Yes," she nodded. "It's all well. But what news do you have of Patrick?"

"We have some information, Mrs Wilson," answered the woman cop as the trio entered the house, steering around the excited dogs. "Would you like to sit down, Ma'am?"

Suddenly dry in her mouth, Marjorie flopped onto the sofa and reached for the warmth of her pets lolling by her feet. She feared the worst, and they gave her strength.

"We traced Mr Wilson to West Waterfront," Harding said with a hint of victory in his voice. "However, the hotel name, 'Horse and Carriage', appears to be something he cooked up."

"C-Cooked up?"

"No such place exists."

"What? But I sent...sent him a package there...um...his shaving kit...and some other odd bits." She brushed a curl from her forehead and bit her trembling bottom lip, recalling that day in the post office three months ago.

"Yes," agreed the lady cop. "The post office has corroborated that as well, but we don't know if it reached him because they marked it as '*discard if undelivered.*'"

"I didn't...."

"I know," replied Harding and added with a shrug, "Looks like everyone in our little neighbourhood was out to give him a hard time for how he treated you, Margie."

The lady cop touched Mike's arm. She was aware of her partner's affection for the young, battered wife, but they were here on a formal mission and couldn't get personal.

"Anyway, what is established is that he *definitely was* in West Waterfront," Mike continued, "for at least two days and staying quite close to the post office in the town. There are only two hotels in the locality. One is called the Atrium, and the other, Gotham Place. We drew a blank at the Atrium, but at Gotham Place, we found him."

"Found him?" Marjorie stared, astonished at both officials in turn. They were not making sense.

"Well, I mean, we found details of him." Mike hesitated and chose his words carefully. "Gotham Place is an upmarket meeting point for high-class pimps and prostitutes."

"Oh!" Marjorie's cheeks coloured.

"He didn't check in the day he arrived in West Waterfront," Mike added. "But his mobile phone triangulation evidences that he was in the vicinity for about two days. Then, for some reason, he turned off his phone – quite naturally, the service provider could not track his device after this."

"We have evidence from Gotham Place that he checked in two nights after he left here," the lady cop added. "He left his room the following morning and never returned."

"But didn't you say they found him?" Marjorie breathed. "Is he in custody for some felony? Can I see him?" She rose, but Mike Harding requested her to sit down again.

"No, Margie. When we said we found him, we didn't mean alive."

Marjorie collapsed into her seat, her face white and her lips dry. Her delicate nostrils flared, and her eyes were big. She only said, "No! That's impossible," and buried her face in her hands.

Mike Harding couldn't understand the devotion this lovely, docile creature could have for a louse like her husband.

"Bloody good riddance," he thought insensitively. "I'm sorry, Margie," he added insincerely. "We received this wire from the West Waterfront Police." He held up a sheet of paper. "Are you okay for me to read it to you?"

Marjorie glanced at him. Her breathing was shallow. Her face was red, and her eyes were big and bewildered. She gritted and nodded.

"You okay, Mrs Wilson?" the lady cop asked.

Marjorie nodded again. "I'm fine. I'm fine."

Mike Harding cleared his throat and began to read:

"*The subject, Mr Patrick Charles Wilson, a resident of Richmond, Kingston County, was traced to Gotham Place, 63 Castel Street, West Waterfront. The standard method of mobile phone triangulation was used to determine his whereabouts in the absence of any other evidence. Most likely, the subject checked in at the hotel two nights after arriving in West Waterfront. It remains unknown where he might have stayed before this upon his arrival in the town. Enquiries made around the area of triangulation are negative. No one appears to have seen or spoken to Mr Wilson.*

"*The Gotham place records confirm that he checked in at 7:45 PM with nothing but a small valise and ordered dinner to his room. He remained indoors and did not venture out during the night. It is unclear when he left the next morning, but the cleaning staff found the room empty of any personal effects. There were no signs that it had been occupied, except for a farewell note.*"

"We have a transcript of the note here," said the lady cop gently. "And Officer Harding will read it to you, but let him finish the report."

"*His personal belongings were gone,*" Harding continued reading, "*and the bathroom was devoid of anything that might have belonged to him. The farewell note by the bed was quite generic and did not indicate any cause for alarm. It contained the following message:*

"'*I've been unfair and horrible to you. Let me go.*'"

Here, Mike Harding paused and re-read the part privately, and a glimmer of satisfaction appeared in his eyes. Marjorie was still staring, flabbergasted at him, her mouth dry and agape. At her feet, her dogs rolled for her attention, grinning with their red tongues lolling out.

"Did he write the note?" she asked, breathless.

"Well," Harding hesitated because more gruesome details were to follow. "There is no name or signature at the bottom. However, the hotel staff confirmed no one visited him the night he checked in. So, while circumstantial evidence indicates he was most likely the author, you will obviously be required to identify the handwriting. But, Margie," Harding's voice was low and gentle. "There's more. Let me read on."

Sitting up erect and hugging her belly, Marjorie nodded. Her heart pounded, and she wanted to cry.

"*Gotham Place registered a case of bad debt with the police,*" Mike Harding continued reading from the report. "*Since the note did not precisely point to a suicide, the police followed up the complaint from the angle of petty crime. The subject had not registered his mobile phone with the hotel. As a norm, the hotel also does not insist on the information because of its reputation. So, the subject remained uncontactable.*

"*Last Tuesday at 02:35 AM, during the high tide, the police were called to the pier to investigate a body that had washed up from the sea. It was an unidentifiable white male between 35 and 45 years of age. Apart from advanced decomposition, the face and body showed severe signs of mauling by aquatic life. A post-mortem exam confirmed that the subject was likely dead and in water for at least ten weeks. His height, estimated weight at the time of death, body structure, and age are very similar to that of Mr Patrick Charles Wilson. However, this is only circumstantial as there was nothing by way of identity found on the body, except for a smudged bill on the letterhead of Gotham Place and a mobile phone, destroyed by the action of saline seawater.*

"Whilst we cannot confirm that the subject is Mr Patrick Charles Wilson, we are certain that he stayed at Gotham Place, which coincidentally corresponds with Mr Wilson's Mobile Phone triangulation.

"The corpse will remain at the Corona's mortuary for seven days from the date of this letter. If unclaimed after this, it will be cremated by the county.

"We remain at your disposal."

Mike Harding glanced at Marjorie's white face and hesitated again.

"I know this will be too much for you, but we recommend making a trip to West Waterfront to identify the handwriting on the note and the body," he said. "I will be happy to drive you, Margie," he added hopefully.

Slack-jawed, she could only stare at him.

"If it is him, which we think is likely, you may also pick up his personal effects," added the lady cop.

"Personal effects?"

"The mobile phone, the note, the letterhead from Gotham Place, his clothes, shoes...."

Marjorie broke down.

"Mrs Wilson," the lady officer said, gently touching her shoulder. "I'm sorry. I'm so very sorry."

"I'm not," Mike Harding whispered in her ear as he rose to leave and nodded as Miranda Curtis flounced in. She removed her bug-like sunglasses and glanced from one face to the next.

"Why are we so grim this evening?" she demanded. "And shame on you for making my daughter cry, Officer!"

"'Evening, Mrs Curtis," he greeted, his face reddening. "I believe we have some news about Mr Wilson, but we will let Margie tell you all about it." And he smiled, glancing at the young woman's emotionally charged face, unsure if he read profound grief, absolute relief, or extreme joy in her big, tear-filled eyes. Regardless, he knew where he would spend his free time from now on. Marjorie needed a man to love her, and he would be that man.

Once they had gone, Marjorie resolutely dried her eyes and told herself she needed to keep occupied, or she would become wildly overwhelmed. She proceeded to the outhouse to cook her dogs' dinner, and her mother followed her in curiosity.

"I'm not interested in Patrick for the moment," the older woman said dismissively. "I hope he never returns. But what did the doctor say?"

Marjorie blinked, and the tears came again. She glanced down at her flat belly and wondered what she would feel when it became swollen with the life it now carried. She reached into her pocket and extracted an envelope, handing it to her mother. It was a lab test report.

"I am to go to West Waterfront as soon as possible to identify a body," she replied in a low voice, her face white. Turning towards a large fridge in the corner, she extracted a hunk of meat. "I might as well do it tomorrow," she whispered and added unnecessarily, "But after I go to the market and stock up on some mutton or beef for the dogs. I'm out as of today."

Smiling faintly, she brought a knife down on the mass of frozen meat with a force that might have surprised her mother. But that lady, intent on examining the report, hooted and gathered her daughter to her, beaming with joy and pride.

"Congratulations," she cried. "Fourth time lucky? Get this pooch dinner done quickly, darling. I will not say I'm sorry that your husband is most likely lying in a mortuary now, but I will say I am over the moon to know that I'll be a grandmother soon....oh goodness!" she then cried, pointing to a large knife standing in the corner. "Whatever is that horrid thing doing here? Cruel, cruel man!" she gasped, now peering at a smear of dried blood on its keen edge. "I wonder what he killed and gutted."

Marjorie observed it from the corner of her eye and felt a pang but remained silent, intent on her task. How long had it been there undetected? Three months?

"Oh! My! God!" she thought. "How did I not notice it before?"

She shuddered at a memory, and a wave of nausea nearly overwhelmed her. Steeling herself, she gave no sign of her unease and continued with her task. But, deep down, Marjorie's relief knew no bounds. So did her joy! She brimmed with it and struggled to hold back her tears. Trying to mask the twin emotions, she carved the thawing meat with a spasm of violence.

"You were a horrible, horrible man," she told her husband in the secret of her mind. "This is the last of you, Patrick Charles Wilson," and she loaded the meat into the pot with a serving of vegetables.

"Do you have to go tomorrow?" her mother asked. "I mean, if the man's dead, then what's the hurry?"

"I have to go, Mother."

Miranda shook her head, vexed.

"Well then," she replied, sighing in resignation. "I hope it won't be a wasted trip, and I'll be able to say *'good riddance to bad rubbish'* tomorrow."

Her mother left her, and Marjorie, happy to be alone in her supreme joy, slid down the shed's wall in relief. She cuddled her womb and glanced at her dead husband's knife. She'd have to clean it and put it back in its place – or better still, get rid of it along with all those other horrid swords and axes!

She was a free woman now, she realised. Free from battery, tyranny, and abuse. And free from the fear of the law, too. And it was all because, three months earlier, one of her dogs affectionately licked a wife-beater's face, only to get punched in return. That single act of violence brought into sharp perspective the unprovoked whipping she had suffered and the degrading sexual abuse. Exploding with rage, she cracked her husband's skull open with the heavy buckle of the same belt with which he had lashed her.

It was opportune that he had a penchant for large knives and choppers, for she had spent the whole night hacking him into pieces and cleaning up the mess. It was suitable that he worked in refrigeration too. Storing so much meat would have been a task, and a beast like Patrick would have stunk to high heaven.

It was also most convenient that her dogs didn't care about the type of meat they ate!

And posting the mobile phone to a phoney address in West Waterfront? Sitting on the floor, hugging her belly, Marjorie glanced up at the pot of ghastly stew on the boil and sighed in satisfaction. It was probably still in its bubble wrap envelope with a shaving kit, drained of charge and lying lost forever among all the post office discards. Reading up on all those crimes solved by Forensic Science was worth her every effort to keep abreast with criminology.

No, she hadn't gone wrong anywhere. There was no dead body, and the murder weapon was now strapped around her waist. The only witnesses were two dogs with enormous appetites and the inability to talk.

Tomorrow, she'd testify to a farewell note and identify a poor West Waterfront stranger as Mr Patrick Charles Wilson. This unfortunate unknown was a stroke of Divine

Intervention, she realised with a prayer of thanks in her heart.

And perhaps on the drive back, she would study Mike Harding's face and decide if he was really handsome or not.

XIV

The Vendor on the Eastern Queen

Even as Jottu counted his money with an avaricious wish that he could double it with a snap of his fingers, he found himself flying and luggage of varying shapes and sizes surging towards him like pebbles churning in a fish tank. As he flew out and was tossed like rubble with the dead and dying, he told himself that the line was indeed jinxed!

But he had a business to run, he vaguely thought, barely avoiding a mass of steel that flew over his head and crashed somewhere; he didn't bother to look.

Two hours earlier, he'd had only thirty seconds. Thirty seconds to pick up two plastic woven baskets – one filled with eight thermos flasks and the other with assorted biscuits, buns and samosas – and board the express train that had halted at the Ratanpore station.

Ratanpore station! Like a speck in a string of beads, it lay about a hundred miles down the line from the sprawling metropolis of Gawhati. It was so insignificant that the

Eastern Queen favoured it like an afterthought with a thirty-second stop!

It was half past three in the afternoon when he swung into the train. Being such a tiny station, folks boarding and deboarding in Ratanpore were few. Besides, the Queen ran interstate, from Gawhati in the East to Madras in the South, almost 900 miles away. Jottu cared less for the South. The climate was hot, the rains were torrential, and the people spoke a language he could never understand. His world comprised of Ratanpore and Maggad, the next station, another tiny grain in that string of pearls with which the Eastern Queen decked herself.

Jottu hopped into the carriage vestibule, bags hanging from both arms and swung into the second-class compartment. The Eastern Queen impatiently chugged out of the station and soon picked up speed again. In three-quarters of an hour, it would scream into Maggad, the next station, where he would disembark and catch the local 'Five-Forty' back home to Ratanpore.

His face, etched with eternal disgruntlement, grimaced. The Five-forty was perpetually late! Five-forty was a misnomer. It should have been called the Six-thirty or even the Seven-O'clock!

This was his daily routine – Ratanpore to Maggad and from Maggad back to Ratanpore on various trains that graced the stations with their thirty-second stops. With sixteen years of this grind behind his belt, one could blindfold Jottu and plant him in any of these two stations, and he'd accurately identify where he was purely by the sounds and smells of the place.

Today, despite the grimace, he was pleased. His pocket bulged with money from all the afternoon tea, coffee and snack sales he had made. The morning selling had been good, too, and when he went home to lunch and to replenish his supplies, he had deposited a wad of notes with Jamuna, his wife.

Until last year, he had sold only tea and biscuits to the travellers on the local trains, sluggish caterpillars that coiled through from the prior station to Ratanpore and from there to Maggad. Then, when the government introduced the Eastern Queen Express, there was greater churn – people from the south came east, and people from the east went south. The East likes its tea. The South loves its coffee. Jottu added three more flasks, all containing coffee, and stocked more paper cups, content to watch his clientele litter the station with the empty receptacles rolling in the railway breeze.

As he wobbled with the train through the compartment, he buzzed, "Tea, tea, coffee, coffee, biscuit, bun, samosa," pausing at various berths and handing out tiny cups of steaming beverage. Down the aisle, he hustled, conducting his commerce with alacrity – watery tea or coffee sloshing in small paper cups; samosas oozing oil on square pieces of newspaper; biscuits powdering in their wrappers, and buns as hard as a stone. Slurping sips on puckered lips and crumbling patties between munching teeth matched the 'chuga-chuga-chuga-chuga' of the racing train as Jottu rocked from berth to berth. By the time he returned to collect his payments, jingling his baggy pants with change and neatly folding all the currency notes in his pocket, tongues were working double time to dislodge bits of bun, biscuit or samosa between teeth, and hands were dusting crumbs from laps, littering the smooth blue floor of the train.

Back home in Ratanpore, Jamuna had told him to come home early that evening. It was his eldest child's birthday.

She was turning fifteen and had been adamant about having a party with all her friends. Jottu scowled at the idea as he collected his payments. Only the silliest people had parties with cakes and candles when they turned a year older. Now, he mused as he walked along the compartment, it was reasonable to 'sweeten the mouth' with a 'jalebi' or a 'cham-cham.' But a party? Nonsense, he thought. And what an example to his twelve-year-old, or his youngest, a spoilt little creature of only eight. He clicked his tongue. Why couldn't Jamuna give him sons like a good, dutiful wife?

The Ratanpore doctors had said something absurd about he being responsible for that little detail.

"Ah! How can that be?" he had argued with an exasperated lady doctor. "Am I the one swelling up with children?" And he tapped his stomach, where a tiny paunch was beginning to show. That was eight years ago. Now, his tummy was more prominent than Jamuna's had been back then.

"No more children," she had said, content with their three girls. She combed and ribboned their hair and sang to them in the evenings. They talked nonsense at supper and giggled at romantic scenes and dialogues on television.

He scowled at the thought of the television. It was an evil thing, he concluded. It put all kinds of ideas into his daughters' heads. That's how his fifteen-year-old got the idea of a birthday party!

Still, Jamuna was not a woman to be trifled with. Like most wives, she was submissive, keeping her head down and attending to her wifely and motherly duties, but when she dug her heels in, she was unwavering. She was clever, too, he reluctantly conceded.

"Instead of travelling on the trains with your bags," she would suggest when in the mood to dispense advice, "set up a stall in the station where you can stock so much more than tea, coffee, biscuits and samosas. It would save you the trouble of travelling in the trains. You could learn some maths too," she'd add with a palpable hint at his dull brain for the subject.

The idea was logical, but a woman advising him on running his business was not! Why would a woman want to dip her nose in his profession? Her job was to nuture and nourish. His job was to protect and provide.

He glanced down at the two baskets and frowned. This time, it was not because of his giddy-headed fifteen-year-old or his wife's sense of commerce. It was because his flasks were still full. Of the eight packed tightly in the basket, three were empty. There were still another five, full, hot and steaming. Two flasks contained tea; the remaining were the southern pick-me-up that the 'Madrasis' preferred. The other basket was still loaded with biscuits and samosas. If he jumped off at Maggad and returned to Ratanpore, he would incur a loss, especially on the drinks and the samosas. One could always sell dry food the next day or the next week, but tea, coffee and samosas? People liked them fresh!

Still, it was the fifteen-year-old's birthday!

"Aaah!" he slapped his head to remind himself of one universal fact. "Birthdays come every year. What's so special about this one?" With this reasoning, Jottu made up his mind.

He wouldn't jump off at Maggad. He would ride the rails to Karmalok, another hour away.

Well, he thought as he swayed towards the end of the noisy compartment to wait by the door and count his earnings; Karmalok was a bustling station. The folks there enjoyed a nice, steaming cuppa with a biscuit crumb or a samosa. The thermos Flasks would keep the beverages hot till he got there, and he'd make a killing on the platform. From Karmalok, he'd catch a bus back to Ratanpore, or if he were lucky, he'd get that local Five-forty. That damned train was always late, anyway!

But travelling to Karmalok was always a jinx for him. The last time he'd extended his journey, the train had stopped midway and had waited nearly an hour because a connecting track ahead needed to clear. Jamuna wasn't happy when he got home. It had been late, and she had been up, keeping his dinner warm.

"Why did you have to go there?" she had asked in a loud whisper, afraid to wake the girls. "Besides," she added with a pointed glare at him, "It's not as if you don't make enough on your usual route."

"More is better than less," he grumbled.

"If more is important to you, take my advice and set up an eatery at our station," she snapped. "That way, you won't have to travel so much."

"Go to bed, woman," he replied testily. "I don't tell you how to manage your kitchen."

"Oh! So that's your stand, eh?" She rose in a huff and added sarcastically, "Tell me, dear, what is your profit today?"

He didn't because he couldn't. Jottu had failed maths in school, and it was sad because another time, when an oily-faced and corrupt collector had caught him travelling on the express line without a ticket to Karmalok station and fined him five times the amount, Jottu ended up losing even more because he couldn't multiply fast enough, and consequently received lesser change than what he was owed.

The Maggad to Karmalok trip was always unlucky for him, he told himself with a scowl. But then, so was Jamuna. She had given him three daughters when he wanted sons. How unlucky was that? Still, he reasoned as he sat in the vestibule and watched the land sweep by like a watercolour distorted by a fat, moist brush, what was bad luck? It was only an alignment of the stars, and the stars came out only by night. Now fleecy clouds clumped upon the moving horizon like thick white smoke from a giant's cigar. Daylight dazzled in the pale skies like lovely princesses offering flowers in the temple. The stars had been subdued! The trip to Karmalok wouldn't be a jinx. He would fling a bundle of notes in Jamuna's face and challenge her to calculate his profit! Besides, he recalled an old friend's sagacious opinion:

"There is no such thing as a jinx. We are all the products of our choices."

With this thought, Jottu was resolved. He would continue from Maggad to Karmalok, finish his sales and find his way back, either by the bus or on that Five-Forty.

The Eastern Queen roared into Maggad Station, her wheels screaming as she entered the line between the platforms, stopping for the customary thirty seconds. Then she picked up speed again and roared like a furious cheetah toward Karmalok. The sky was bright, and the air smelled of business. Jottu decided that the child would have to blow out her candles and cut her cake with her mother, sisters and all those screeching school friends. What a waste of money. Who was going to make good those expenses?

Not Jamuna. Not the silly fifteen-year-old or the easily swayed twelve-year-old. And certainly not the spoilt eight-year-old.

Who else but he?

Hunkered by the door, he watched the world whizz by and tried to calculate his earnings till now. Behind him, the humdrum of conversation revolved around cricket – India playing South Africa and winning by six wickets. What a waste of time, he thought. Cricket! Someone threw a ball, someone else hit it, and a third person ran to collect it. And then that whole thing was repeated. To what end? At least tea gave one's taste buds pleasure. Coffee stimulated the mind. He tried to calculate his profit in his head again, made a mess, and gave up. Jamuna would tally his accounts tonight. She would gasp and proclaim him a hero!

And then a sobering thought flashed in his mind. Why were numbers so hard for him?

But he would never find an answer, at least not at that time. The conversation behind had changed to politics, and one man was vocal, speaking in an accent that suggested a 'Madrasi.' Jottu listened for an instant, couldn't understand the argument, and reached into his pocket to count his bundle of notes.

"Ah!" he thought. "I wish I were like that famous magician, P C Sorcar. I'd snap my fingers and say clever words, like '*Hocus Pocus*,' and my notes would double like milk boiling over."

In that instant, an explosion tore the compartment open, and steel, luggage, limbs, heads, blood, and gore hurtled towards him.

There was chaos and devastation – five bogies had derailed, crumpled like biscuit wrappers and flung upon the tracks like refuse. Ahead, another train had rammed into the Eastern Queen because of a faulty linking of the rails and its own coaches were scattered like match sticks – some were on fire!

The air around was rank with death. At least a hundred bodies lay between these two devastated strings of metal like crimson rice – some whole, many quartered, some groaning, some twitching, and many still.

And then the wails and the moans and the howls came to Jottu like a second explosion as he sat up dazed, shrugging off something warm and bloody from his shoulder. He stood up, swayed and surged forward, staggering over the dead and the dying, running over tracks and falling headlong. He rose, ran and fell again, this time into someone's arms.

"Why are they shouting," he wondered with a twisted face. A trickle of blood rolled down the side of his cheek, but otherwise, he appeared to have no other wounds. He felt a little deaf, somewhat traumatised and very confused as his hand reached for his pocket. The cricket commentators seated behind him had been ground to a pulp. The man adept in politics would never reach Madras alive, and many of Jottu's customers had had their last drink or snack served up from his thermos flasks and his basket of nibbles.

But Jottu, collapsing into somebody's arms, only racked his brains with a single thought:

"Where are my bags? I've gone and lost all my money! Oh! Oh! Oh!"

The trauma of losing that lovely wad of notes was too much. As Jottu fainted, his last thoughts were of Jamuna, her business model and a silly fifteen-year-old's birthday party. And, of course, the earnings he might have still had if he had gone home to cake and candles instead of travelling on a jinxed line.

XV

Sarah-Ann Prescott

"I have a little girl too, you know?" said old Mrs Prescott.

She was sitting in a straight-back chair, hugging a large handbag with her ankles clamped together. Her white upper feet puffed out of her very red pumps; these perfectly matched her white dress with large red rose prints. Even her thin smear of red lipstick fitted with her attire faultlessly. What might not have sounded right was the reference to the 'little girl.'

The woman was undoubtedly senior – a fact given away, least of all by her neatly permed silvery-white hair. Her small, pale face was crisscrossed with age, with powder and rouge on cheeks that sagged colourfully in a scribble of pink lines.

Sat before a table, a younger woman turned, glanced once at her and knitted her brows. Then she turned back to a passive priest reclining in his seat. He only smiled understandingly, pulled down a large book from a shelf behind him and proceeded to make an entry within it.

"So, this date is confirmed, then?" he asked, and the young woman nodded. "Congratulations again, Sally," he added, and his eyes lit up with a smile. I've often seen you and him in church on Sundays, so I'm unsurprised that you two want to settle down together." He added, "He's a good man."

Sally nodded, but there was no blush on her face. She was old enough never to feel self-conscious anymore. A few years over forty, the decision to marry had happened because her father had passed away the year prior, and she had realised, with the newly added responsibility of her old mother, how lonely the senior years could get. With Ryan Conway, her stout friend of many years, by her side, she was hopeful that things would be a lot easier.

The priest continued to refer to his large register, copying from certificates she had given him. Sally watched him, her hand forming a tight ball in her lap. Behind, the old woman continued to sit straight in her chair, waiting for the proceedings to complete.

"Sarah-Ann Prescott," she muttered. "That's what I named my little girl."

The priest looked up from his writing; Sally turned, too.

"She was baptised here in this very church," she added, staring at something on the floor. Then her small eyes rose in their nests of wrinkles, and she looked straight at Sally. "Were you baptised here too, my girl?"

"I was," Sally replied with a small sigh. "Many, many years ago."

"Oh! My Sarah-Ann must be around here, running about." The old woman peered from the window where children played in the church compound and pointed a shaky finger forward. "I can't see too well, but I'm sure she's there, prancing around with them. Such a sweet, lovely child, my Sarah-Ann."

Sally glanced out the window at the frolicking children and then at the old woman. With a sigh, she turned back to the priest and asked:

"Can we get a slot in the morning, Father?"

"Well," said the priest, shaking his head. "We have a morning wedding at 10:00 AM but nothing in the evening. I can only give you the evening slot."

Sally bit her lip, hopelessly considering the proposition. A morning wedding would have meant lunch for their guests, which would have left the evening for her to be with her mother and, of course, her husband. She couldn't leave her mother alone, not even for a single night.

"I had an evening wedding," the old woman offered from behind, and Sally rolled her eyes.

"Did you, Mrs Prescott?" The priest knew the old lady well. With a smile, he added, "This church? I'm certain I wasn't born yet at that time."

"Born yet? Sarah-Ann is definitely born," Mrs Prescott appeared confused for a moment.

"No, Mrs Prescott," said the priest patiently. "I must have not been born yet when you were married in our church.

"Oh, yes, indeed," she replied. "That was so long ago. I got married in this very church. My little girl, Sarah-Ann, was baptised here. She had her First Holy Communion here, too. We had white ribbons and flowers."

A light gust of breeze blew in from the window, and Mrs Prescott's rose-patterned dress fluttered over her knees. Her red smear of lipstick stretched into a thin line, showing a neat line of pearly teeth, but the priest could not tell if she was smiling or gnashing. It was always tricky with old people, he realised.

Sally appeared to know because she thinly smiled back – a strange smile mixed with a wave of hopelessness, impatience and restrained frustration.

"And then we all went home in a white carriage drawn by four white horses," added Mrs Prescott, still grimacing or smiling – the priest could not tell. "Her father had a bit of a task that day – one of the horses dropped dung, you see, right here on the church grounds, and we were all quite embarrassed."

Sally huffed loudly and almost glared at the old woman. She had a long day to go. Once the church work was done, she had to get back home to give her mother her medication. The old woman's constant interruptions and musings were not helping.

Outside, the children still played in the sunshine, and one girl twirled about, laughing as four or five others formed a ring around her. The old woman glanced outside, too, and pointed a quivering finger once more.

"My Sarah-Ann," she said.

"Will you be quiet, please?" Sally said at last with exasperation. "I've tons to do, so it will help if you remained silent for a while."

The priest shifted uncomfortably. He was a young man and would have liked to tell Sally off – the old woman was only trying to make conversation, to be friendly while she waited. But his better judgement told him otherwise. Sally's life wasn't easy. She had an ailing mother to support and worked long hours each day. Fortunately, she worked from home – a saving grace because of her mother's condition. Besides, she was much older than him, and he understood – he knew that her life was hard. Her widowed mother was not easy to manage, and being an only child made matters even worse. Her decision to marry, albeit late, was a sensible one. Not only was she marrying her best friend, but she was marrying a man who understood her predicament and would form that additional support Sally needed now.

But then, poor Mrs. Prescott was only trying to be friendly. She loved to chit-chat with friends, strangers, anybody. She hadn't had an easy life, either. Recently widowed, all she had now was a memory of her little girl—her Sarah-Ann Prescott frozen in time.

Still, the last thing he wanted was these two women bickering in his presbytery. He quickly diffused the tense atmosphere with a question to Sally:

"Would you need the church to arrange a choir, or do you have your own?"

"The church, please, Father," replied Sally.

"Okay." He then pulled down a massive, red Bible, opened a page and showed her a few readings. "Choose any one of these from the Old Testament," he said, "And any one of these from the New Testament. And..." he moved the ribbon, opening another page. "Here are the suggested Gospel readings. I would recommend the Gospel of the Miracle at the wedding in Cana, but you have others you can also choose from. Would you be making Wedding Mass booklets?"

"Um," Sally hesitated, wondering about the extra expense. "I don't think so. No."

"We had booklets," chimed in Mrs Prescott. "When my husband and I were married, we had little books with all the readings so that friends and relatives could follow the service. I remember our Gospel reading was John 2, verses 1 to 11 – the changing of water into wine at Cana."

"You remember that?" Sally turned and asked incredulously.

"Of course I do," replied old Mrs Prescott. "Sarah-Ann's father had insisted on it. He must be somewhere around..." She appeared confused as she strove to find him among the children in the sunshine outside. Then, giving up, she cheerfully continued, "We were only married a few years ago, my girl."

Sally sighed softly again, turned to the Bible and angled her neck to note all the suggested reading chapters to show her fiancé from her Bible at home. Then, after she had completed all the other formalities, she made the nominal payment, thanked the priest and rose, stepping out of the small presbytery.

Mrs Prescott remained where she was, looking out of the window and unsteadily pointing her pink finger in the general direction of the frolicking children.

"My Sarah-Ann will be married too someday," she whispered.

The door opened again at that moment, and Sally popped her head in, looking at the old woman with some vexation.

"Mum," she called with a deep sigh of endurance. "Are you coming?"

XVI
Desdemona

"Hey dude," said Rory Williard to his friend, Mike. "Seriously, it would have been nice if Callie came too. But then, I heard that Zane Marshal is in town."

Mike Rowling, seated in the car as it sped over an endless ribbon of country road, twitched his brows in the slightest wave of annoyance. This was the second time Rory had mentioned, with not so much as even taking his eyes off the road, that his wife should have also joined them on the weekend trip.

Zane Marshal, on the other hand, was new flavour!

Mike let it pass. Zane was Callie's ex, and he didn't want to waste his thoughts on him. But he understood why Callie had been reluctant to accompany them, and Rory was hardly the man he wanted to confide in. Callie's reason for not joining them was Rory himself, and Mike, sucking hard at his cigarette, gave it some thought. He and Rory had been friends for years, but something about this impish, smiling and affable man began to abrade like sandpaper! It was his effusive chit-chat, Mike told himself. Rory could never contain his mouth. Conversations were monopolised with books he'd read, movies he'd seen, people he'd met, foods he'd tasted, cars he'd driven, and bikes he'd crashed. It was always, 'hey-dude-did-you-know-this' and 'hey-dude-did-you-know-that.'

Estranged from a wife Mike had never met, yet still living with her under the same roof, Rory was a father of two teens. Still, Mike knew his friend led the free life of a bachelor – the different girls hanging on his arm and his words were proof enough.

Outside, the country snapped by like an everlasting smudge of blue, green, orange and red. The valley dropped away to the silver sheet of a lake, like a mirror under the afternoon sky. The slopes were dotted with May trees, red and orange, and the foliage was thick and juicy, rejuvenated by the rains of the preceding weeks.

Mike realised he was sucking on a spent cigarette, and the acrid taste of burnt tobacco on his tongue made him grimace. He flung it out of the window with a soft oath of disgust and glanced at his phone, wondering if he should call his wife. Why was he suddenly uncomfortable?

It wasn't only Rory Williard's volubleness. There was something else, too, and Callie had mentioned it to him. A gleam shone in Rory's eye, particularly when he dove into a tub of roguishness and wished to flirt surreptitiously. It was an evil gleam which suggested...no declared:

"Callie, if you hadn't married this dumb arse, I would have made you mine."

Mike had laughed this off when she told him.

"Cal, I've known him for years. Rory Williard's a talkative chap, terrific with the ladies, but he's harmless."

"I'm uncomfortable when he's around," came her persistent reply. "Call it a woman's intuition."

"Just because of a photograph?"

"Yes."

"I don't think he meant any harm when he messaged it to you, doll."

"I think he meant that and only that," was Callie's stubborn response, and she recalled the day. "Remember that evening he came home with his brother, Sean? You and he had stepped out to pick up some beers, and I was chatting with Sean in the meantime. When I learnt that Sean and Zane Marshal were school-mates and we were marvelling at how small the world is, you chaps turned up, and he wanted to know whom we were discussing. So, Sean told him. That night, Rory sent me a photograph of Zane. Mike, who does that?"

"You're upset because Zane's your ex, that's all." Mike, trying to sound nonchalant, played it down.

"No! I'm upset because that's over for me, but Rory wants to bring it up again for some devilish reason. I sense something dark and murky deep in him. The desire to sow the seed of discord. To try and stir up something long dead and buried."

"Callie," Mike laughed at her reddening face and button nose. "Callie, my darling! How could he have known about you and Zane?"

"Because when Sean told him we were talking about him – Zane, Rory immediately said, 'Oh! Zane and I are pretty tight, dude.' And then he blatantly asked me, 'Weren't you two going around?'"

"Yeah, I heard him say that," Mike admitted, "And it was somewhat unnecessary. But look, I don't think he meant anything by sending you that photograph. Honestly, I'm not bothered."

That wasn't entirely true, and thinking about it now, Mike almost winced. Zane was a tall, good-looking chap, open, affable, and fun. He had a knack with the girls; it wasn't surprising because he was well-off – an only son and well-placed professionally. A tall man. A well-built man. Every woman's dream come true. But as is with all things that are too good to be true, Zane had a roving eye. And it was this that had nipped a budding love between a young Callie and that tall, handsome man nearly ten years ago.

Ten years! That was long ago. Mike and she had been married half that time, so this had been no rebound. Yet, suddenly, why was he now unsure?

Because he wasn't what the world would call a wealthy, affluent or successful man? Because he wasn't great on looks or physique? Because it was impossible that Callie would pass up a vibrant, fabulous man for a nobody like him.

Callie said she never regretted it. As far as she was concerned, she swore that marrying Mike Rowling was the best thing ever for her. The thought put him in a better frame of mind for a moment. He relaxed and watched the countryside whipping by as Rory expressed his views on the subject of afforestation. He hardly listened because somewhere at the back of his mind, a shard of discomfort raised its ugly head, and he became thoughtful again.

"If you don't like Williard coming here, I'll tell him so," he had suggested to Callie that day.

"Mike, I don't want to separate you from your friends," she replied. "He's not a regular visitor, thank goodness! But whenever he pops in, I'd like to keep to myself."

"Okay."

But why? Did Rory know something about that dead love affair that he didn't?

Regardless, Callie backing out from this trip wasn't surprising. What was annoying was that Rory wanted to remind him that his wife had stayed home. And somewhere, during that voluble thesis on afforestation, the conversation circled back to wives and significant others.

"You know my wife?" Rory said. "She hates being alone at home. We don't talk anymore...she does her thing, and I do mine, but my word! She hits the roof if the kids aren't home by a specific time. When we were newly married, she did the same crap with me, but now..." he shrugged. "I like it like this. We have our own lives, and it's good."

Mike buried himself in the map on his phone, trying to find a back road that would lead them further into the hills.

"But Callie's such a sweetheart!"

"Hmm?"

"I was saying your wife's a sweetheart."

"I know. That's why I married her. I suggest we take the next left." Mike gestured with his phone. "The map indicates it's a good road, and it loops right into higher forests and hills."

"Any town along the way? We're down on cigarettes."

"One in the hills."

"Okay, let's do it," Rory agreed, and when the turn came up, he swung left. "So," he cleared his throat. "Did you know Zane?"

"Who?"

"Zane, dude. Zane Marshal. Callie's..."

"A little," Mike replied. "I met him once or twice when Callie and he were a couple."

"He's a big, muscular, good-looking chap. One of the nicest dudes I've met. Married now with two boys, but I hear that he and his wife are heading for Splits-Ville."

"The town," said Mike, peering at the phone and expanding the image on his screen with his thumb and fore-finger, "appears to be a forest outpost. The road 'dead-ends' there."

"Forest Outpost? Do you think they'll put us up for the night?"

"From the map, it appears a biggish place. So yeah, I think there'd be some sort of accommodation."

The men drove on, Rory lapsing into silence for a spell, but from the corner of his eye, Mike felt he was being furtively observed. He sighed and looked out as the country rushed behind him. The valleys dropped away as they climbed into the hills, gunned up switch-back turns and loops of fantastic beauty.

Callie-Callie-Callie. Why was he so uncomfortable? Because Rory Williard had brought up Zane Marshal? Because he secretly felt second to Callie's ex?

"I spoke to him yesterday," Rory's voice crashed into his thoughts. "He's in town."

"Who?"

"Zane Marshal."

Mike shrugged, but his brows knitted even more. Was there any reason he needed to know that Zane was in town? He strove to stay calm. They were alone on this weekend trip. Getting into heated words wasn't a good idea. Mike held his peace and only tried to smile. But he made a mistake when he said:

"Can we change the subject?"

Rory Williard construed it as something else. He slowed the car, halted it and turned to his friend. "Dude, I'm sorry. I didn't know. I mean, I know Zane fooled around with some other babe, and that's why Callie broke up with him, but are they now trying to get back together?"

"Huh?"

"They aren't?"

"Williard, I have no clue what you're driving at." Mike may have wanted to sound perplexed, but the hair on his neck prickled.

"Hey, sorry, dude! I thought you had some suspicion."

"What suspicion?" Another tiny lie.

"Okay-okay-okay," Rory smiled, and his eyes gleamed. "No need to get testy."

"Williard, can we please stop talking about my wife?" came the tight request.

"Okay, dude," Rory began to laugh, "But don't get hot under the collar. I think your wife's a gem, and I care for both of you. Zane's my good friend, but he has a way with women."

"Williard, crank her up and let's move," Mike ordered. "We have at least two hours of driving before we reach this outpost." His voice was toneless and carried a hint of a warning. Rory only chuckled and started the car.

"You're one of the nicest guys I know," he remarked. "If someone had said that to me, I would have turned this car around and driven home just to see what my wife was up to!"

"We are all nice guys," Mike said, fighting his growing anger. "Until we become not-nice."

"Yeah. But I heard they were pretty close."

"Who?"

"Callie and Zane."

Mike lit a cigarette. He didn't like this conversation. He didn't want another man talking about his wife.

"Williard," he warned again. "Callie's my wife. So can we please not talk about her?"

"Sure thing, Dude," Rory shrugged. "I'm only trying to watch out for you —Zane's in town. Callie's decided to forego this weekend trip and is alone at home. Aren't you worried if she's okay? I mean, my wife, when we were newly married, would have called me a hundred times by now asking when I'd return."

"Mine isn't the clingy type."

"I'm only trying to say that Callie must have made some prior plans with friends, no?"

"Possible. I don't control her."

"Hmm. That's why I tell everyone you're the nicest dude I know," Rory said. "A little dumb, but nice."

"Williard, what the deuce do you mean?"

"Nothing, dude. Nothing. Old flames are allowed to catch up, huh?" Devilish glints in his eyes accompanied his words. "Even if they've married other people?"

"Okay, that's it," Mike seethed. "Stop the car, Williard. I've had enough of this."

"Hey-hey-hey!"

"Stop the damned car!"

There was an uproar within that steel box, and if the birds could speak, they would have described a machine coiling up the hills, charged with the sounds of men arguing. They would have gossiped about how the steel box paused and how a man jumped out with his rucksack. Then, the car started up and sustained its climb. The man walked briskly downhill and continued in this manner till a forest escort going in his direction stopped and picked him up.

Mike jumped off in the next town and caught a bus rolling out, heading for the city. Deep inside, he was a man on fire, his heart scorched by suggestions and suspicions intensified by five years of denial.

Zane-Callie-Zane-Callie.

Photograph-anger-Zane-Callie.

Count me out if Rory's going to be there-Zane-Callie.

I prefer to stay home-Zane-Callie.

I have two books to read-Zane-Callie
You have fun-Zane-Callie.
Zane-Callie-Zane-Callie

With tears flooding his eyes, Mike bought himself a ticket home. He would reach around midnight and in perfect time, too, to perhaps catch an errant wife and her ex-lover. The shadow of Zane had always loomed in his mind. He had only buried him because it was simpler that way, but now he was going to bring everything out into the open. He was going to ask Callie, tell her and toss her into a cesspool of shameful guilt!

Driving up the winding country road towards the forest outpost, Rory Williard lit the last cigarette, but it tasted horrible. He spat it out and swore, stopping his car by the side. He had been happily married, too, but somewhere between work and babies, he and his wife had drifted apart. One had shrivelled and gathered into herself. The other had expanded towards the pleasures of life. Now, all that was left was a diluted, watered-down version of him, and he was jaded. Mike and Callie's simple love had brought his complicated life into startling perspective. Happy couples infuriated him. Besides, he always wanted to teach Callie a lesson. She was too snooty for his liking!

Back in the city, the ex-boyfriend Zane Marshal checked himself once in the mirror and left his hotel room, whistling into a blushing sky. He and one of his many past loves were meeting up, and he hoped to get lucky. A wife was somewhere with two sons. He cared little for her now. She had gone too fat after their second boy – like a rubber band stretched so far it had lost its elasticity. Flabby, lumpy and loose, she had become an embarrassment. An orb, a mass of moving flesh. He shuddered, pushed her from his mind and reached to ring a familiar doorbell. As a pretty face answered the door, he shouldered inside and disappeared.

And in a small house in that same town, Callie Rowling was getting her dinner ready. She loaded everything into the oven, set the temperature and curled up on the sofa with a book to read. She was happy. In some ways life had not happened as she had dreamed. But she was content with her book, the ticking of her oven timer and the marriage band that gleamed upon her finger.

XVII
The Trap

Norma didn't care for the van anymore. It rolled out of the driveway and disappeared into a clump of trees on the road beyond. She barely even noticed it now. Two years ago, she had been very interested in that same side door where the van would park twice every day, but Pete, her remarkably intelligent husband, had forbidden her from nosing around.

"You keep to your side of the house," he had cautioned, indicating the kitchen and the prettier positions of their home. "And keep those bakes going," he added. "The smell is delicious and brings all those hungry tramps and gypsies from across the green."

And so they did. The aroma from her oven wafted from the window like ambrosia from the very kitchens of Heaven, and no matter what one said about the baker, the cakes were delicious.

"Worth dying for," Pete would guffaw, making some silly attempt at a tasteless joke.

Norma was ramrod thin, pinched and angular. Her lips were like two white lines stretching east to west on a long, wrinkled face framed by scanty iron-grey hair. Despite the daily baking, the delicious aroma of her kitchen, the sunny garden and the wide-open country outside her window, Norma's face appeared starved, wrinkled and old – perhaps a little mad, too! Her eyes were black and held a crazy light in them – which turned brighter when she went down to the basement to where her clever Pete worked. Obviously, there would have been a time when she was young and perhaps softer and prettier, but Pete could never tell, and neither did he care. He had been married to the woman two years now, and her affinity to the oven had made him rich!

The sound of the engine faded, and Norma turned to the oven. After two years, the coming and going of the van and all that happened by that side door held no more interest for her. It was a daily thing, and she fell in with the routine the same way the hands of a clock shift with its ticking.

Now, she had completed her daily bake of deliciously smelling cupcakes; about a dozen of them were upon the window sill, cooling. If her mood permitted, she'd ice them or sprinkle little sweets on them. But most of the time, they tasted just as good the way they were and were polished by the hungry gipsies in no time.

Down in the basement, she heard the chainsaw at work, and her thin lips struggled into a smile. Tidying her thin hair in a knot no larger than a pebble, she glanced at her reflection in the window pane and decided that she looked fine.

The chainsaw stopped wailing for a moment; Norma crept down and peeped around the door where, in the yellow gloom, Pete worked tirelessly behind a curtain of thick polythene. It was terribly stained red now, but later in the day, she would soon wash it down, and the tainted water would trickle away into a drain in the corner. The smell all over was heavy and nauseating, so terribly unlike the kitchen upstairs, but for Norma, this was as typical as the sun rising each morning and setting each evening now. She watched Pete in awe – what a fantastic coroner he had been in his day. Though he had now given up active practice, he still performed the job informally, tirelessly and almost zealously.

In deep fascination, she watched him carefully carry, in his gloved hands, a purple-red body part...a kidney? Norma had no idea. She wasn't allowed any further from this door where she now stood when Pete was at work. She wasn't allowed anywhere close to him when the chainsaw was running. It was too dangerous, Pete had said.

"Just bake your cakes and keep 'em coming," he would add when he finished, shucking his bloody apron and flinging it into the wash.

Now, he carefully placed the red, jelly-like thing in a blue box – a special blue box meant for safe and hygienic transportation - and sealed it shut. He placed this on a table by the side door and turned once more to the table behind the stained polythene curtain.

"Would you like some tea, dear?" she called, and Pete sent a bloody thumbs-up sign in her direction. Then he turned to the table again, lowered his mask to prevent splatter on his face, and the chainsaw screamed again. Norma bolted upstairs, almost throwing up.

The cupcakes would have cooled by now, she mused, racing into the kitchen, and most likely, a couple would have already been devoured. Her prediction was accurate – not because Norma was clairvoyant, but because this had happened so many times before. On the board in the window, four of the treats were missing, with only crumbs in their stead.

Peering out of the window, her face split into a struggling smile. Two urchins sat there, devouring her cakes. When they saw her peering at them, they rose in alarm, but she beckoned to them quickly with another two cakes, one in each wrinkled hand.

"Come, take," she said with motherly kindness that contrasted with her pinched face. "Don't be scared."

Hesitatingly, they rose and approached the window. They were strong, young teenagers radiating with health despite the dirt on their faces and grime in their nails. Their clothes were tattered – the boy's trousers were held in place by a string. The girl's blue skirt was now brown with muck and patched in many places.

As they snatched the cakes from Norma's hands, she gestured toward the kitchen door, inviting them to step inside. Two large pairs of dark eyes stared at her, their lips circles of wonder.

"Our big brother," stammered the girl. "He cames this way yestidey and nary returned to camp. Mebbe you seed him?"

Norma shook her head.

"Many come by," she said. "I love to bake, and those who come by have a bite or two." Her eyes dulled as she tried to recall the tramps that came by yesterday. Yes, there was a young man – a healthy chap with a whipcord frame and an arrogant face. Pete was overjoyed to see him.

"You like the cakes, don't you, my dears," she said instead and invited them inside, leading them to the table. "Let me put some icing on them, and you'll like them more." Layering the tops of the cakes with pink, blue, red and white sprinkles, Norma placed them before the children. She sat down and placed her chin on her elbows.

"Eat," she said, her thin lips stretching further into a smile.

The two didn't need a second invitation. The delicious cakes with their colourful icing were too tempting, and they reached forward with enthusiasm.

"Do you live with the gipsies?" Normal asked softly.

The girl, supposedly the elder, nodded with her mouth full. She was a middle to late teen – her tattered clothes did little to hide the budding youth of her body. The boy, a little younger, looked no better. His cap was too large for his head and almost hung over his nose. Down, his toes peeped out under torn shoe-uppers.

"And is this little fellow your other brother?" As Norma asked her next question, she placed another cake before the boy. He didn't appear too interested in the conversation between his sister and the woman. He only ate with gusto and devoured cake after cake placed before him like a hungry child who had no idea where his next meal would come from.

The girl nodded and nibbled at her treat. She still glanced around suspiciously as the distant wails of the chainsaw sounded. Lash, their older brother, had set out yesterday with his flute, hoping to play a tune or two in the marketplace and earn a few coins. He hadn't yet returned, and it wasn't like Lash to stay away from the camp for so long.

"Come, Manfri," she tugged at her younger brother's sleeve as she rose to leave. "Come."

"Finish your cake, dearie," Norma urged, leaning forward to catch her hand. "Don't be scared of that sound. That's only my husband. He never stops working. Besides," she added, struggling to smile again. "In the basement, I have a room full of old clothes and shoes...and quite a few that would fit a pretty girl like you."

At the woman's words, the girl hesitated. Glancing at her dress and frowning at the tattered, worn fabric, her first thought was whether she would find something warm in that room of treasure! With this thought, she sat down again, reaching for her cake.

"We ain't got no coin to pay, marm," she murmured.

"Pay?" Norma echoed with a dismissing gesture. "Nonsense!"

When the children had just about finished their snack, Norma picked up a tray and placed two cakes, a cup of tea, a small bowl of sugar, and a jug of milk on it.

"Now," she said. "Pete, my husband needs his evening tea and cakes. So, follow me and don't let that horrible sound frighten you. As I said, it's only him at work." She smiled in excitement. "He's a very clever man. As for you two, help yourselves to the clothes and shoes – I'm sure you'd like a new dress, dear and you, young man, a pair of boots?"

"With buckles?" asked the boy in excitement.

"With buckles, with laces or even those fancy ones with zips."

For the first time, the girl smiled.

The van sounded in the driveway again, and Norma knew they had come to collect the blue box. They'd access the basement through the forbidden side door, pick up the box and leave the way they came, never knowing that she existed. That drove a smart of pain into her, but Pete had always told her that she was the one who kept the forbidden side door working. The thought brought a twinge of satisfaction. Pete had the brains – but she had the bait, and it worked like a charm each time! She knew they paid Pete for whatever the blue box contained and sped off to the hospital to give someone a new lease of life.

Pete was so noble!

The children followed her downstairs, still munching on the last remnants of their cakes, and when the chainsaw screams commenced again, louder this time, the girl didn't seem so startled as before. She only tried to muffle the screeching sound by covering her ears and grimacing at her brother as he laughed, trying to guffaw louder than the chainsaw. Norma only placed the tray on a small table by the entrance to that awful, nauseating room and ushered the teens past an adjacent door.

"Go on in," she said. "There are tons of clothes there. Take what you want."

As they peeped into the room of assorted clothes and shoes, the girl's eyes fell on something familiar and she cried out in shock:

"Why, that's Lash's jacket…"

Whatever else she wanted to say ended abruptly in a yell of bewilderment as she felt her body catapult forward towards the articles and her brother toppling untidily on top of her. She fought him away and turned towards her captor, but Norma had already clamped the door shut.

"Pete," she cried above the sounds of the chainsaw. "Two more in here."

The sounds of the chainsaw ceased briefly.

"Told you those cupcakes are to die for," came a grunt and Norma, with her pinched face and iron-grey hair, smiled terribly.

Then the wailing commenced again, and Norma went upstairs to the kitchen. Tomorrow, she'd bake another dozen cakes and leave them in the window to cool.

It would be nice to snare another passing tramp or two who took a fancy to her cupcakes. Adults were preferred, but children were not that bad!

As the evening came on, Normal would close her kitchen for a while to help wash the basement while Pete took his repast of tea and cakes. It was also her job to get that incinerator running, consign all the discarded body parts, bone, tissue, and matter to flames, and wash the blood away so that Pete's work area remained neat and clean for the next set of living donors.

They now screamed and banged futilely on the door of the room full of old clothes and shoes – clothes and shoes of the donors who had gone before them!

XVIII
Nana's Gift

My doll only stares now.

There was a time when she was more than a doll; she used to talk, walk, sing, cry, and even laugh. Dark hair, full of curls, eyes flecked with green, and rosy cheeks—Nana, my grandmother, gave her to me at my birth, and I couldn't live a day without her. On my first day of school, in a crisp new white uniform, a red pre-tied necktie to proclaim to the universe that I now belonged to the Sacred Heart, and shiny black shoes, I should have been excited to step into a world of new friends, ABC and one-two-three. Instead, I only bawled to be parted from my doll, clinging on doggedly and sprouting tears till one teacher called me a sissy, tore me away and led me to a classroom of other little girls gaping, confused at me.

She was much, much more than the doll she is now. She was my friend, the heroine of every little story I imagined. I talked to her, fought with her, confided in her, loved her, hated her and slumbered with her. Everywhere I went, she was with me; I liked to think she held my hand, leading me through bookstores, toy shops, clothes departments, and fruit and vegetable markets.

My lovely, beautiful, dark, curly-haired, rosy-cheeked friend!

As I stare at her, alive from my past, a relic of my present, I recall how her batteries never seemed to die. They went on and on and on. I believed she, too, did all the things I did. As if by magic, she'd brush her teeth, change her clothes, comb her hair, and read, sing, talk and play. She'd lie with me on the cool grass, gaze up into a summer night and count the stars, and I'd wonder how many of them shone in her pretty green eyes.

Sometimes, we would go to the park together and sit among the flowers and fountains, where the big, black bumble bees hummed and poked into pollen casks and frightened the children playing around. They'd shriek and scramble towards us for protection and marvel at my friend, standing in awe of her lovely, smooth skin and rosy lips. They'd want to touch her, hold her hand and pretend she was theirs.

Nana told me I must always cherish her and that I could never have another like her. But, the simple joys of our childhood and the interests of adolescence are two ends of a spectrum. Far more opposing is the rat race of adult life! My friend, the one I could never be parted from, was now right down on my list of priorities. Like a dress out of fashion or shoes run down at the heels, I had left her to herself, blushing in awkwardness if someone happened to notice her.

"Let's get going," I'd urge. "We can't be late for the movie."

I might as well have locked her in my box of old dolls and toys and stored her in the dusty attic because I didn't need her anymore. I loved and wanted her where she was, but I didn't need her like I did as a child.

And her batteries ran out sometime between when I stopped needing her and now! Sometimes, I tried to charge them, and they worked for a little while, but the inner mechanics had turned old and jammed. After a point, no amount of charging would bring the life back into my friend. As I turned from child to adolescent to 'Who's that pretty young thing?' to 'What an iron-willed woman!' she crumbled from rosy cheeks and glossy curls to pallid decay, incoherent speech and total a-kinetics.

Sometimes, there's a moment when I detect a twitch in her eyes, like a blip on the radar of life, like a shooting star in the darkness of the sky, but that is only one of the last struggles of her mechanics to turn a cog somewhere deep inside.

My doll only stares now, and Nana, who gave her to me at my birth, isn't around anymore to tell me what to do. She was Nana's doll, and Nana looked after her well and kept her beautiful for me. Nana told me that one day, my doll would give me to my child, as she had done! But with the passing of time, the bitter winters and the boiling summers, my rough play, my harsh words, my cold shoulders, my doll deteriorated to silence and solitude.

She's become a stranger lying on a hospice bed, staring glassily at me when I try to get her attention and call the one name Nana taught me to call her.

"Mum."

XIX

Black and White and Red All Over

Even though he was alone, Charles 'Chippy' Sloane felt a sense of tranquillity. It was a long time since he'd felt this way. He hunkered beside the decorated Christmas tree, dwarfed by its awesome height. To the ceiling, it reached where an angel pointed a plastic glare down at him as if forbidding him to come any closer. He lowered his gaze quickly. The angel reminded him of his sister's husband, and the glare brought snide comments, open taunts and full-blown fights to uncomfortable recall.

Tinsel of silver and gold streamed like the sparkling skeins of a mythical tree, incandescent under the action of the winking lights - red, blue, yellow and green. Baubles of every colour and size imaginable hung like perfectly spherical glassy fruit on plastic bristles tipped with white splashes to resemble snow. One red ball reflected a rosy fish face back at him, pulling his nose forward and elongating his forehead - Chippy didn't want to look. He didn't like his face, piscatory in the shiny curved surface or not. Quickly, he set about his task because he had little time. Five gifts lay on the carpet beside him, waiting to be wrapped. He reached for the first - a children's Bible - he covered it in red paper dotted with Santa heads and candy sticks and wrote on the card:

"To my darling Samantha - your tree needs a nicer angel, and you are best fit to take its place. Have a happy Christmas, and keep me in your prayers. Your uncle, Chippy."

A tear threatened to smudge his writing, and Chippy breathed sharply. He loved his darling Samantha. She reminded him of his own daughter, now living with an estranged wife who wanted nothing to do with him. Samantha, too, was somewhat estranged, he realised. Her father frowned each time he tried to chat with her. Giving it a little thought, Chippy relented. He would, too, if a man who'd done time wanted to befriend his little child. But Steve wouldn't have to put up with him anymore, Chippy told himself with a calm shrug. He was taking care of that tonight.

Settling a ribbon on the gift, he lay it at the foot of the tree and glanced once more at the critical angel.

"Chippy, you're a coward," it seemed to tell him. "You couldn't bring yourself to fight your wife in court. You think you've got the guts now?"

Did he have the guts? He raised his eyes towards the apology for a Christmas Tree topper. It stared him down - the more he looked, the more accusing was the glare!

"Bah!" Quickly, he returned to his task. "Focus! Focus! You haven't got all night."

Quite true. He didn't have all night, and he certainly wasn't Santa Claus. He had small gifts to give to the family who had taken him in when no one else would. They were attending Midnight Mass at the chapel down the street with the customary cake and wine party to follow at the club. Veronica, his sister, had pleaded with him to go with them, ignoring the knitted brows of her husband.

"Come on, Chip," she had begged. "It's been six months since you've been out. Who cares about the world? I know you're innocent. Steve here believes it too."

Steve only grunted. Believing something was one thing. Being convicted and serving time was another. He had a reputation to uphold. Besides, he and Chippy never got along.

"Let's move, Ron," Steve told his wife, tight-lipped. "We are getting late. Sam! Where's your coat?"

They hurried out, leaving Chippy alone in the house; Veronica had kindly given him the little cottage at the back when he had finished his time. Chippy decided he'd have to tidy up the place before the night was over. It was a nice thing to do. But then, the mess he would leave would always be there. Wouldn't it?

He clicked his tongue and reached for the second gift. It was a pair of black T-Strap Dance shoes. He'd paid an arm and a leg for the patent leathers because there was a time when Veronica loved to dance. She still did, if only Steve would ask her out.

"Ask me out? My husband?" Veronica's peals of laughter shook the tiny cottage one evening as she put up curtains to make the place more habitable. "Chip, you might as well hope for snow in hell!"

"But I saw an amazing pair of ballroom shoes, Ronnie," he had argued. "Just the right fit. And you dance so well!"

"You are hopeless," she said, pulling his cheek affectionately. "You'll be alright here?"

"You bet!" He had nowhere else to go. "Thank you for having me here, Ron."

She only nodded and left. He knew Veronica backed him to the hilt, but his world was darkness, disgrace and shame. He had suffered seven years in prison for a stacked crime of beating his wife. She had served him divorce papers while he was in jail and was now remarried after cleaning him out of everything. Nothing remained now except the gifts he wanted to give and the rest of the night.

The shoes reflected the twinkling lights from the tree. He placed them in their box and wrapped them with lacy gold paper. On the card, he wrote:

"Your feet were made for dancing, and these shoes were made for you. See you sometime, my darling sister."

He couldn't find words for the third gift. It was a broad silk tie, proudly tiled in blue and grey and meant for a corporate mogul. The tie exuded power; with a subtle silver sheen along each tile when pointed towards the light, it was sure to raise the wearer to a position of self-assurance and superiority. Chippy only wrapped it in white paper dotted with motifs of tiny red and gold candies and wrote on the card:

"Steve, for the next 'Cake and Wine' at the club. Happy Christmas, mate!"

The fourth gift brought tears - it was all he had left of Amanda, his little girl snatched away with cold disdain and insensitivity by a wife who had once loved him but had now moved on with her divorce lawyer. It was a small picture album of their marriage, Amanda's birth, her first adventure with solid food, her innocent relationship with an old doll and many other memories. With a smidge of guilt that he hadn't fought hard enough for at least visitation rights, he breezed through the pictures, precious and familiar; yet distant, smoky and awkward. His wife had sought a restraining order against him when he finished his time, and out of the smarting ignominy of facing a stern, dough-faced judge, he had honoured the injunction and stayed away. Their marriage picture presented pride, arrogance, beauty and joy. She, beautiful and joyous, in pure white and smiling as she cuddled against his strong shoulder and he, all arrogance and pride, in full uniform - tassels, medals and lanyard, and the five-star insignia of the Commissioner of Police!

Ex-Commissioner of Police, he told himself with a snap! Because, now, he no longer carried the title, having served seven years for the charge of beating up his wife. He had never laid a finger on her, let alone beat her, but she had come armed and ready for battle, painting him with a brush that made the entire police force blush. Then, out of the blue, she brought an additional accusation that he had abused their infant daughter!

Commissioner Charles 'Chippy' Sloane closed the picture album with a snap, and a gust of cool air trapped between the thick cardboard pages flapped into his face. He wrapped it up quickly in red paper designed with white hearts, placed a bow on it and wrote:

"Remember your dad, Amanda, my girl."

The last item was a flat cardboard box; another smaller but thicker case made of polished wood lay beside it, but these didn't appear to be gifts because there was no wrapping paper left. Chippy glanced once at the plastic angel, still blazing her eyes down at him and smiled calmly.

"Yes, these last two boxes are for me," he told it. "So, stop glaring at me like I'm such a despicable man. I aim to go with whatever dignity I have left."

Settling the gifts under the tree one last time, he picked up the two boxes and quietly left the house, going to the back where his little cottage stood, away from the street and shrouded by leafless shrubbery. A few lights twinkled on the naked branches, like skeleton fingers playing with coloured pearls - Veronica's sweet attempt to make Christmas a happy time for him.

"Dance, Ronnie," he said to an image of her in his mind. "Your feet were always made for dancing. And Steve, if you cannot take a hint with that tie, you ought to be jailed!"

Entering his home, he placed the articles on a chair and tidied up the living space, the small dining table, a writing desk, his bed and finally, the kitchen, where the sink had only one coffee cup. With a grunt of satisfaction, he looked around and found everything in order. Then standing before a small fireplace, Chippy undressed, opened the flat box with unwavering fingers and retrieved a crispy khaki uniform embellished with all the insignia of a high-ranking and decorated police officer. Donning it, he stood to attention before a thin, long mirror by the door and nodded at his reflection in grim approval.

Then he reached for the polished wooden case, opened it slowly, and his eyes glittered at the police-issue semi-automatic handgun sunk deep in hard black foam packing. It was a heavy grey pistol with a 9mm calibre, a licensed copy of the Browning Hi-Power. Beside it was a 13-round detachable magazine, containing a lethal 9mm Parabellum in the foam.

Chippy's experienced fingers reached for the weapon and snapped in the magazine with one smooth, fluid movement. Then, standing to attention, he muttered, "Happy Christmas, you old loser. Your last seven Christmases were like a black and white movie. A splash of red now is all that you need," and stoutly raised the pistol to his head.

Had the bells not been ringing at that time to hail the best and sweetest time of the year, a gunshot might have cracked the night and brought all festivities to a close sooner rather than later.

Veronica and Steve would return home before dawn, carrying a slumbering Samantha and note the four additional gifts under the tree. The shape of the box would instantly tell Veronica of its contents, and she would smile with sisterly affection. Steve would fidget with the white wrapping of his present in flushing mollification and whisper under his breath:

"You, old son-of-a-gun!"

The angel would stare accusingly as if to complain about the cheeky suggestion that she be replaced by a little girl, Samantha, who couldn't even keep her eyes open on Christmas Night!

And far away, in another town where the night was chill, but the fireplace was warm and fuzzy with sleighbells ringing, tinsel glittering, presents, music and cake, a little child named Amanda would fall asleep in the arms of another man, whom she now called daddy.

XX

The Abilene Rose

Dylan Conway couldn't feel his legs.

He'd heard her familiar voice seconds before seeing her and stood up, stunned, almost in disbelief. It was, indeed, Sally – tall, straight-backed, dark-haired and brown-eyed, with a touch of fire that only he knew could blaze into anger or passion. They could also fill and overflow, he told himself. A wave of relief spread through him as blood pumped back into his knees, and he marvelled at the colour in her cheeks, the little glossy curls bouncing on her forehead and her red, parted lips now sucking in deeply when her eyes fell on him. A sense of exhaustion also filled him, and his breath caught. The last three years on long cattle drives came hurtling back – drives that no sane man would ever have done, all in search of her.

Now here, north of Abilene, on a spread watered by the Clear Fork of the Brazos, he'd found her nearly 300 miles from home. Happy, laughing and chasing a rambunctious toddler who looked remarkably like her – and like him – she ran into General Prescott's study and stopped short, gaping into his bewildered face.

"Conway," said the General. "Meet my niece, Sarah – Sally for short."

Dylan snapped back into the present. The letter she had left when she ran away three years ago and their marriage licence were in his pocket. Around his neck, on a rough leather thong, was her ring; he had carried all three wherever he went, like a torch – his only connection to her and all that kept his memories strong during those long nights when he lay, staring up at the sky, listening to the lowing of bedded cattle, thinking of her.

He reached out instantly to take her proffered hand. She was his wife, Goddammit! You don't shake your woman's hand. You grab her, toss her into the air and twirl her around. The little boy, stoutly planting himself between them, challenged him with innocent blue eyes to come closer, and Dylan lost sensation in his legs again. A lump formed in his throat. This was his boy! And then, with a sliver of irritation, he silently admonished himself.

"You ain't the only one who's had it tough," he thought. "Stop thinkin' 'bout yourself and appreciate what she's been through."

He knew it hadn't been easy for her. On those many long cattle drives – planned only so he could accomplish the dual task of selling beef and searching for her, he had stumbled upon a little convent north of Dallas where the nuns had spoken of a Sally Conway and the twin boys she had sweated to deliver and keep alive. One didn't make it and was buried in their cemetery. Her life had been hard, too, but she didn't look one bit weary now. Her lovely eyes shone, and her laughter was like music.

"Sally?" he mouthed, unable to take his eyes off her. He couldn't believe how incredibly beautiful she was, and he fell in love again as any man with blood running in his veins would. Three years he had spent loving the thought of her, the shape of her, the sound of her, the fragrance of her, and now she stood before him in the flesh. Something burst inside him – his life? For her, for that little man at her side, a toddler of perhaps two years and showing all signs of rebellion. He remembered a boy like that. If his father were alive, he'd have stories to tell!

"Well, well," General Prescott chuckled, easing the tension. "You ain't the first to go all slack-jawed, Conway. Colonel Morse, my neighbour, is right smitten, too. I ain't never seen a man more in love than that young fella."

Dylan came crashing back to earth. He glanced at his wife, tilting an enquiring eyebrow at her, and she raised her chin proudly, holding her squirming son.

"It's nice to meet you, Mr. Conway," she nodded, her voice soft and husky. "Uncle Dave, I'll be in the valley." Picking up the child, she ran from the room.

"I worry for her, Conway," the General sighed, glancing at the doorway where Sally had vanished. "She doesn't talk about it much, but from what I know, she has a husband. Won't speak of him and won't hear anything said about him. Sally's had her share of life – from scrubbing floorboards to washing pots in some frontier eatery. She had that boy over at a Convent north o' Dallas. Colonel Morse is sweet on her. Well, I ain't complaining. My niece needs a husband and her son, a father."

Dylan Conway flushed and hoped nothing on his face gave away his discomfort. His heart sank. Why would a girl want to travel 300 miles away from her family to live with a husband from whom she'd run away in the first place? They had been apart for three years! That was more than enough time for any marriage to break. Wouldn't Sally welcome the attention of Colonel Morse and perhaps dream of marrying him? Wouldn't she want to marry someone who wanted her? Wasn't it logical that she'd like to live next door to her kin? And who was he? He asked himself irritably. An Oaky boy looking for the wife he had pointedly told he didn't love. He had only married her because he had lost his head one night during a fight when she had been his housekeeper. He couldn't remember what they fought over – a man and a pretty girl, but he remembered he had kissed her to silence her. Then he kissed her again, and that had led to other things. Dylan had married her because it seemed the right thing to do. But those days, he had been seeing a woman called Ursula Unger and wanted to keep the union a secret till he broke the news to her.

Sally's farewell letter had said that they had never had a marriage, and in a way, it was true. In that brief two months of their time as man and wife, he had rarely seen her, keeping his distance and spending his nights with the cowboys on the range. The letter burned in his pocket. *"I could have stopped you that one time we were together,"* she had written. *"I didn't. The reason is simple. I loved you. But then, we never had a marriage."*

Never had a marriage! He'd spent three years looking for her. From that morning, when they were camped twenty miles north of Fort Worth, when he and his riders were starting up the final lap of their drive and he'd realised that she had left him until now. Dylan Conway had but one goal from that day on—scour the whole of Texas for her, find her, tell her he was sorry, push the ring on her finger, and bring her home.

"If this ain't a marriage, then I don't know what is," he told himself resolutely.

Tomorrow at dawn, he was starting back for home. Home? When she'd left, it was a burnt-down shack, the work of scoundrels who wanted to run him off his range. Now, he had built it up again with solid stone. It was bright and airy, but most of all, it was strong. He'd built it with Sally in mind – a place to raise a family. Dylan glanced towards the door where she had hurried out with their son. The little face might be Sally's, but he saw himself in those eyes and in the raw courage to stand between him and his mother to protect her.

General Prescott was still chuckling. "Well, I done never seen Sally so flustered in all my life," he remarked. "You ain't so bad yourself, Conway. Any man who can drive cattle 300 miles gets a tick in my book. Is it true what they say? You're lookin' for someone?"

"Yeah."

"You found him?"

Conway smiled uncomfortably, signed the bill of exchange, collected the check and shook the General's hand.

"Mebbe."

Riding out of the yard and into a small valley where summer flowers bloomed, he noticed a pony chomping desultorily on the lush grass and a woman hunkered on a rock, watching her son bounce about with a wooden pistol. His mouth went dry when she turned to him and stood up. Dismounting, he walked to her, searching his heart and mind for something to say. He glanced at the boy pointing the pistol at him and gurgling 'bang-bang', and he pretended to die. That eased the tension because Sally smiled for an instant. He looked into her big brown eyes.

"I found the convent," he managed to say, and she glanced curiously at his face. "Yeah! Folks say it's foolish of me to drive cattle for miles and miles, but it was the best way to...to look for you, Sally."

"Why?"

"Why? You're my wife."

"No, I'm not," she whispered. "You loved her. What happened, and our marriage was a mistake. Besides," she looked up, and her eyes flashed defiantly. "The nuns told me that if a marriage is not consummated, it's not a marriage."

He smiled as a memory came back. "Wanna fight now? We can consummate away among the flowers."

Sally caught her breath and turned away, biting her trembling lip. She had almost forgotten how tall he was, but his intense blue eyes were never far from her memory. Rough, rugged and sometimes arrogant, she instantly fell in love with him the day Ursula Unger, his lady love, brought her to his ranch as a housekeeper. Only he didn't even notice; if he did, he kept it buried under rough orders and fiery arguments when they disagreed about something. This was the man she loved, the man she could never forget, no matter what, and whose sons she bore. The memory of her loss came back and brimmed her eyes. Swallowing hard, she gained control of herself and turned back to him.

"You never loved me," she whispered. "You loved her."

"Well, I don't think I can size up to a man like Colonel Morse," he said reflectively, appearing not to hear her. Then he bluntly asked, "You love him?"

A blaze of anger fired her cheeks, and as her lips trembled, she raised her chin defiantly. What did he think of her now? That she'd run away from a man she'd give her life for so she could welcome the love of another? Suddenly, she wanted to hurt him and bring down his arrogance a notch or two.

"Why not?" She shrugged with a coolness she didn't feel. "He's kind, and he's attentive. He's asked me, and I might say yes soon."

Conway's face hardened with fury, but he also had a remarkable way of remaining calm. Still, the hurt creeping into his eyes was evident.

"That's fair," he muttered thickly. "Sally, for whatever it's worth, I'm sorry."

"For what?"

"For what happened between us."

She laughed, and her eyes filled with tears. With a groan, he reached out to gather her to him, but she stepped back, warning him off with a gesture.

"Come home, Sally," he begged in a low voice. "Come home, please."

"Home?" A smile dawned on her lovely face, and despite her tears, her eyes lit up in merriment. "Home? To a burnt-down cabin with a makeshift roof and canvas for curtains?"

"Home," Dylan said again. "In whatever shape or form."

"Colonel Morse has a huge place with a fence and a garden."

"Colonel Morse ain't ridden the trails for three years and travelled across the whole of Texas to find you."

"He's not crazy."

"He's not your husband."

Sally raised her chin again, but her lips trembled, and tears brimmed in her eyes.

"You love her, Dylan," she whispered. "You were meant to be her husband, not mine."

He laughed harshly and looked away as tears swarmed his eyes, too. Finding Sally and knowing he could lose her again hurt like never before. Yes, there had been another woman, but all of that had died when Sally ran away to give him his freedom. But she was right. He'd read enough of the law to know that a man and woman separated by three years could never be termed a husband and wife, especially when he had only been with her the day before their marriage.

"Listen, honey," he said gruffly. "I'm staying in town at Finnegan's place, and the boys and I leave at dawn tomorrow. If you think you can live in a burnt-down cabin with a makeshift roof and canvas for curtains, and if you believe this marriage is worth it, meet me tonight. Otherwise..." he reached into his pocket and extracted their marriage licence. Pushing it into her hand, he added, "It's yours – do with it as you please. As for me, I'm married to you and will always be."

Going down on his haunches, he smiled at his son, still trying to shoot him. "What did you name him?"

"Dylan."

"It's a fool's name." He ruffled the boy's hair and quashed every desire to pull the tiny body against his own. Getting to his feet, he mounted quickly. "Come if you think we're worth it."

"To a man who doesn't love me and to a house that doesn't stand anymore?"

"To your husband and your home," he said and rode away.

❦

In the L-shaped saloon downstairs, Dylan Conway's riders revelled the night, whooping to the success of their drive with music, drink and women. He only stood by the window, smoking and gazing into the starry night. His eyes were northward, towards Oklahoma and home. The Polaris twinkled brightly like the merriment he had seen in a beautiful woman's eyes that afternoon. As he smoked pensively, he wondered if he would ever go back to Oklahoma now. It would never be a home without the woman he had built it for. The last three years had made him a restless man, and with Sally not likely to return to him, he felt a deep sense of dejection. A small voice inside him begged him to stay and fight it out – win her and take her home. Another voice told him that love could never be forced. Sally had understood that and had given him his freedom. Besides, she believed he didn't love her, so why would she want to throw in her lot with him now? He groaned gloomily into the starry night at his stupidity. He hadn't even made any attempt to set her belief right.

"Aw, hell with it," he snarled. "You can wonder why you didn't do this or that till the sun don't shine, but that won't change anything."

Stubbing his cigarette, he decided to turn in for the night – tomorrow would be an early day. He'd planned to deviate a little towards the convent to place a few flowers on his son's grave – the thought drove a pang of grief into him. The nuns had said the baby had contracted a fever, and Sally had fought to save him. He had died within three months of his birth. Dylan remembered the little gravestone. It had the name Dean Conway with two dates and four words: *'Hush, our baby sleeps.'*

But his heart warmed at the rambunctious second boy. The rosy cheeks, the big, curious blue eyes, the light hair and the strong little legs filled him with pride. It also filled him with remorse. He would never see his son grow up, he realised; he would never teach him to ride, to shoot, and to rope cattle.

Dylan Conway swore again and made up his mind. He'd send the boys on home. He was going to stay and fight it out. He hadn't spent three years riding the trails looking for his wife to give up so quickly now...especially when he knew she once loved him.

But would she love him again?

A tap sounded on his door, and he spun around, smoothly palming his gun as it swung open. He and his cowboys were new in town—it paid to be careful always. But when Dylan saw who his visitor was, he relaxed with a smile. The buxom Mrs. Finnegan stood in the doorway, her hands on her hips.

"You're gonna drill a hole through me now?" she rasped.

Laughing apologetically, Dylan holstered his six-gun.

With a glimmer in her eyes, Mrs Finnegan added, "You gotta a visitor, Mr Conway—two if you count the second."

From around the doorway, a woman appeared, a sleeping child on her shoulder and a carpet bag in her hand. As Dylan's legs nearly buckled under him, he leapt forward and, in two strides, was by the door, taking the bag and pulling his wife into his arms.

Old Mrs Finnegan left them with a knowing smile, and Dylan closed the door, gazing down at her.

"You came," he breathed.

"Well, I figured I'd have a chance to tell you how to rebuild a burnt-down cabin with a makeshift roof and canvas for curtains," she replied.

"We'll see about that," he smiled mysteriously. "There's no one else, Sally," he added sincerely. "No one else after we married. I love, love, love you, Sally Conway, and I'm sorry...so sorry for what I put you through."

Sally placed their slumbering son in his arms, and Dylan embraced him, sighing raggedly in relief. Then, reaching under his collar, he tugged gently, snapping the leather thong from his neck. She gasped softly when a small ring fell, glittering on his palm.

"Will you give me another chance, Sally? I promise I'll make it right."

"Only if you love me," she smiled. "Otherwise, I'll run away again. I'm quite good at that."

"And I'll find you," he vowed, slipping the ring on her finger. "I happen to be quite good at that, too!"

In the saloon, the cowboys laughed and revelled the night, and tinny music sounded as someone plonked away on a piano. But in one of the rooms upstairs, a man held his wife close, bringing her to little giggles when he softly told her there were better ways of consummating their marriage than starting a silly fight.

XXI

Natural Causes

When they wheeled his body out of the Emergency, Pam collapsed beside the gurney. Yesterday, when I'd waved goodbye to her, she was a petite, slim and beautiful lady, her arms lovingly wrapped around her smiling husband. Today, only thirteen hours later, she was pale, stressed and grieving, her hands trembling over a body that was still warm but cooling with every instant. It had just hit her. Her husband of ten years was dead. With one fell cardiac arrest that dropped him to the bathroom floor, he was dead even before they brought him to the Emergency.

Standing bewildered beside my weeping sister, I placed my hand on her head, trying to console her. I found no words. Sunny, not yet 35, had passed, all in the blink of an eye. He was alive and well last night, chattering incessantly over dinner, so much that Pam had to intervene twice and remind him that he was monopolising the conversation.

How was it possible, I wondered. How could a supremely healthy man, with not even the smallest vice other than smoking, die in seconds? My bewilderment came laced with questions.

I helped my grieving sister and sat her down in the hospital reception till she was able to gain control of herself. Pam's neighbour orbited us, concerned and agitated. He was a tall, nice-looking man who lived on the floor below Pam and had helped bring Sunny to the hospital. Not much older than a boy was my unspoken thought. It was likely he had never witnessed a death before. Sudden, inexplicable tragedies such as Sunny's death would have been bewildering.

As I held my sister's hands and tried to console her, I saw, out of the corner of my eye, a nurse approach and speak to the neighbour. In the distant hubbub of the hospital, the pacing feet, the 'click-clacking' of a keyboard, token announcements and chit-chat, the soft, matter-of-fact whispers were disconcerting.

Pam glanced her tear-filled eyes up as the nurse left the young man. Glancing at both of us grimly, he told her gently:

"They've referred him to the medical examiner for an autopsy."

"Why?" I asked, stunned and stood up.

"The case is a DOA."

"What's a DOA?" I demanded.

"Dead on arrival," the man whispered, his face white. "The police will be here soon."

Hearing this, Pam leaned forward, buried her face in her hands and wept softly.

"He was fine in the morning," I heard her muffled voice say. "He was fine. He went to take a shower and..." She rocked herself and crumbled. I put my arm around her as the neighbour looked on, shifting uncomfortably on his feet. I saw him interlock his hands behind his head and face away, groaning under his breath into a huge glass panel.

Beyond was the hospital driveway where a proud father held up a blue gas balloon with the words, "It's a boy!" and helped his rosy-cheeked wife and little bundle of new life into a car.

What a juxtaposition, I thought as my throat caught.

Two police officials arrived shortly; the very appearance of their Khaki browns and their stoic aloofness, together with that ability to see everything under the lens of suspicion, was unnerving. They spoke with the doctors and nurses, the neighbour and finally Pam. Brisk questions that came like darts, one after the other, left her no time to think, and her responses were mechanical. Then, with the discharge summary, they ordered for the gurney to be wheeled out of the Emergency and into the dark interiors of an ambulance. Pam climbed in mechanically. The neighbour also hopped in beside her. I slid into my car and followed.

With the preoccupation of driving through traffic, I was able to gather my thoughts and think through all that had happened just an hour before. Pam had called - distraught and panicked.

"He's fallen in the shower," she cried. "He's gone limp and does not respond when I call him."

"Is he sweating?"

"I don't know. He is in the shower!"

It was obvious, I gritted to myself. Sunny was a smoker, and I didn't doubt it was what had finally got him. A few months ago, he'd breezed past our home for a coffee and had shared a cigarette with my husband, coughing terribly as he smoked. A bubbling sound erupted from his chest as he laughed away my concerns and tried to allay my fears:

"If my ciggies had to kill me, they would have done so long ago." It was another way of telling me to mind my own business, and I backed off. Pam was an intelligent woman. If I had heard the 'graveyard cough' and been concerned, she would have heard it too - many times and cautioned him, and it would have been her business.

But poor Pam! What a tragedy in the summer of her life! Sunny and she had been friends from school, had spent the wonder of college life together and had appeared happy as husband and wife. Financially, she was very stable because she had a good job and was doing well for herself. Sunny had been the care-free wheeler-dealer, dealing in old cars, with time on his hands to pump weights and run marathons, which was why we were all stumped! How could a healthy man – healthy but for the smoking – die just like that? There was no lengthy preamble of suffering to even hint that the end could be near. Pam never talked about her fears, and there appeared to be no stress or worry.

The office of the Medical Examiner smelled awful. A gaunt building set back in a space of drooping trees shedding their leaves incessantly, it loomed into the morning sky like a gigantic grey coffin. As the gurney disappeared behind a door, a whiff of the inside punched me in the nose and turned me nauseous. The cloying redolence mingled with formalin and weird fruity undertones was ghastly. Pam blanched. The neighbour coughed in disgust and walked away to the space under the trees to sit and wait. Despite the disgusting odour, Pam and I sat in the corridor and were silent for a moment. Then she shook her head as she thought of something and began to weep.

"I heard a bump and ran into the bathroom," she explained softly, staring at the floor. "He was gasping, and his eyes were on mine. They were glassy, and I knew something was terribly wrong. Then he passed out." She glanced her tear drenched face towards mine. "Trish, I lost precious time calling the neighbours and you. I should have called Emergency Services immediately."

"Pam," I squeezed her hand. "I would have done exactly what you did, so stop blaming yourself."

"The cop asked me why I didn't call Emergency Services first," she whispered. "I had no answer. Would he have lived if I'd called them first?"

"The nurse told your neighbour that he was brought dead on arrival," I replied, trying to console her. "He was probably gone by the time you both carried him to the car. Did he work out today?"

She shook her head.

"He ran for about an hour this morning."

"Do you think it caused it?"

"He runs most days, Trish." Pam's voice broke as grief overwhelmed her again, and she crumbled silently. "How did this happen, Trish?" she sobbed. "How?"

The Medical examination took about an hour, and when the report finally came to us, it stated that the death was naturally caused. The report contained technical terms that my eyes glanced over, so I asked the brisk and impatient technician conversing with one of the policemen if he could give me more details.

"MINOCA," he blandly replied. "Myocardial Infarction. He died from a coronary spasm. He was a smoker, wasn't he?"

I turned to Pam, who was still seated but gaping at the technician. Then, she silently broke down again.

Sunny had no family except for an old aunt who lived out of town at an old age home. While still able to remember most things and manage her daily tasks, she was beginning to show signs of fuzziness. Still, the helpful neighbour drove the old lady to the funeral and would also convey her back once everything was over.

"Nice chap, your neighbour," I commented as we sat in my kitchen the next day, preparing for Sunny's final journey. "He's been an immense help."

"Who?" she asked.

"The one who lives below you."

"Steve." She confirmed, drinking hot chocolate from a big mug almost covering her face. It was swollen with grief and chaffed on the cheeks with all her crying. Today, she seemed calmer and rational, and though I did catch her more than once staring out from a window and crying in silence, she was remarkably composed. "Yes," she added. "He's a good sort of fellow and very helpful. Trish," she said, and there was a touch of urgency in her voice. "I'd like to have the funeral over and done with as soon as possible. There's no family, except for this old aunt, though there are a ton of friends, and honest, I am tired of reliving what happened yesterday to every single fellow who calls or messages. And it's summer. The quicker we have the funeral, the better."

Pam was right. In India, the summers are beastly. Here, funerals are completed within a day or two at the most. Besides, keeping Sunny in the mortuary for longer than two days would turn his skin ghastly black and unrecognisable. I know we wanted to remember him as he was in life. Pam, more certainly.

So, according to her wishes and the wishes of the ageing aunt, Sunny was interred at the local crematorium. They were not religious folk- at least Sunny wasn't, and the old lady, I believe, preferred that Pam made all the decisions. With the help of the invaluable Steve, who never tired of all the running around between the various touch points that the funeral demanded, and after the wake and a short ceremony that was teary and heart-wrenching, the poor young man's casket was rolled into the furnace.

Pam stayed with me after this for a while. She was nervous about being alone in her flat – nerves, she called it – and wanted to shift. It was understandable. Those two days leading up to the funeral and for a week after when she'd stayed with me were stressful because I knew she never slept. Often, I'd find her sitting in the window staring into the night, and her face would be pale and pinched with stress. When I'd enter the room, she'd scream in a panic.

"I'm being so childish," she'd exclaim apologetically, and her face would flush red before the colour dissolved into pallidness once again. "I shudder at the thought of returning to the flat and living there, Trish."

About two weeks after the funeral, my sister bucked up her courage and returned to her flat, but knowing she was nervous about being alone, I accompanied her.

"I want to shift and sell the place," she explained. "So I might as well start putting away stuff I don't need or use often. That way, I won't have so much work when I finally need to move."

"It's a lovely flat, Pam."

"Too big."

Quite true. Pam owned a large, roomy apartment with three spacious bedrooms and a kitchen about as big as my whole house put together. Two balconies from the bedrooms faced a large park with many trees, walks and cycling lanes. In the spring and summer, Tabebuias, Jacaranda and May Flowers burst within the foliage in pink, yellow, purple and red clumps. A third bedroom served a dual purpose. Sunny's workout paraphernalia - his assorted dumbbells, barbells, bench press and treadmill lay unattended in one part of the room. In another part stood a make-shift lab, one of Sunny's wild schemes. Pam avoided the room, and I understood why. Sunny spent much of his time here distilling tobacco and extracting 'oil' to make his smokes 'cleaner' and 'safer.'

I stayed with her for a week and helped her pack in preparation for a futuristic shift that wasn't even confirmed. Still, I knew she was looking for a place across the city, and it drove a pang of anxiety into me. Why would my sister want to move far away from family and friends? Fortunately, she worked from home most of the time, so the plan wasn't going to disrupt her professional life, which she now immersed herself in like she had never done before.

"Pam, there are many places around here which will suit your needs," I remonstrated one weekend when she finished conversing with a prospective seller. "Are you sure you're going to be okay?"

"I'm not going to be okay, Trish," she flatly replied. "Every time I sleep, I only think of the day he died and his eyes gazing into mine. But I have to start somewhere, and I have to do it on my own."

"You don't have to," I pleaded, but I knew it was of no use. She had sealed up a carton of personal things and was gesturing for my help to carry it to the corner of the room. "I hate not being able to see you often, Pam."

"You'll get used to it," she laughed. It was a rare moment when my sister turned merry. I smiled, too, and dropped the topic. If Pam was beginning to lighten up at the thought of a new home in a new place, I didn't want to become the wet blanket. "Now to clean up that bedroom," she announced, pointing her nose to the gym cum makeshift lab. She grinned at my puzzled face and demanded that I bring her a carton to fill. "The test tubes, beakers, and flat and round bottom flasks in there only remind me of our chemistry lab in school. Imagine, he had a Bunsen Burner, too!"

I realised Pam was suddenly in a voluble mood, and with a sliver of cheer entering my heart, I let her talk. This was a different Pam—the old Pam—a far cry from the pale, taciturn sister I had lived with over the last two to three weeks.

"He experimented on various tobaccos," she explained as we cleaned up. "He'd extract the oil and collect them in bottles. He said that pure nicotine was not the killer. What killed was the tar and the carbon in a lit cigarette." With a roll of her eyes, she added dryly, "My late husband would never admit that any form of smoking killed."

"True," I said, remaining silent about his gentle way of telling me to mind my own business.

"But," Pam sighed and turned pensive. "I never understood why he hooked up with some pushers."

"Pushers?"

"Yes." Pam began to forcefully pull down an apparatus and load it into the carton. "We'll fling all of this out, Trish. I want none of this. Yes, pushers," she continued. "Weed pushers—powerful guys. They'd come at night with big packages, and Sunny would apportion them according to orders he received from people. Under the pretext of spending time with his friends, he would push the weed for upfront payment, take his cut and pay the pushers."

"What?" I cried, unable to believe what I'd heard. "You were okay with that?"

Pam shrugged and paused in her packing, looking unseeingly at some point on the table. "Initially, it was only to friends - Steve downstairs, for example. Small quantities and small payments, and I was fine, so long as it remained like that. But then bigger supplies came late in the night.

Sometimes, I'd wake to arguments over payment; sometimes, there were threats." Finding a chair, Pam slumped into it and hugged herself, rocking her body as the uncomfortable memories returned. My hand fell on her shoulder, but I don't think she realised it in her distraught reminiscence. "At one point, I wanted out of the marriage because I couldn't take the stress." She laughed cheerlessly at my start of astonishment. "The only problem was if I divorced him, I'd lose heavily- because he has no source of income."

"You hung on," I consoled. "But Pam, do you think these people...?"

She turned sharply up at me. "Which people?"

"These people who threatened Sunny. Do you think they had something to do with his death?"

She glared at me, and her face flushed.

"What makes you think that?" she demanded. "The autopsy stated natural causes, didn't it?"

"Yes, I know," I hesitated. "It's just the suddenness of it." I shrugged awkwardly as she continued to stare at me. "Dying at 35 of natural causes doesn't sound natural to me."

"Trish!" she cried, gaping angrily at me. "Don't stir up ideas, please. Don't stir up ideas when I've just about started believing he's at peace now." Pam's cheeks turned red, and she seemed a different person. "My husband died of a cardiac arrest because of his lifestyle." She waved her hands to encompass the room with all its flasks of weird brown liquids. "This is what killed him," she cried. "Not some pusher who didn't get his payment on time."

I saw the reasoning in her words and nodded ruefully.

"The Autopsy confirmed the cause of death," she added tonelessly. "I don't want to think there might be something else. Now, are you going to help me pack or speculate the cause of my husband's death?"

"Relax, Pam," I said softly, trying to calm her, wondering at the sudden turn of her temper. With a sinking heart, I realised that her moods were swinging. One minute, she was melancholy; the next, sanguine, and then volatile and sometimes even phlegmatic. "You're right. Let's pack this stuff instead and fight about your choice of a new neighbourhood."

I smiled, and she smiled back, and we were friends again.

By the following morning, Trish was in a much better frame of mind. Breakfast was already on the table, and the delicious aroma of coffee in the percolator drove all the drowsiness from my mind. Pam appeared to have worked far into the night because more boxes were stacked up in the corner of the living room. She seemed jovial, humming softly as she scrambled eggs and sizzled bacon.

"Looks like you're ready to move," I observed, sitting at the dining table with my plate of food and inhaling the coffee's stimulating aroma.

"Soon, soon," she replied melodiously, swearing softly at the same time when an egg crumpled in her fingers. "I hate it when this happens," she groaned.

Her phone rang just then, and she hollered to me to take the call. "It would be from one of the movers I contacted last night. I'm calling for quotes."

It was indeed from a packer and mover. The only thing was that they said they did not operate within our city, and I conveyed the message back to Pam. She laughed and said, "Well, I tried two or three last night. Search for Howard Home Transport on Google and call them for me. They sound promising. You'll find it in my search history."

Flicking across her screen, I accessed the Google Search page on her phone and scanned the history of her searches. I found Howard Home Transport, but at least five searches further down, my eyes caught something else which appeared strange.

It read, "*How to cause an instant Cardiac Arrest.*"

At that moment, a message beeped in from Steve, the neighbour downstairs, and it ran:

"*Babe, I found the perfect place for us. Call when you're free.*"

I knitted my brows together and read the message again.

Babe? Perfect place for us? How to cause a Cardiac Arrest? The blood ran cold in my veins.

Pam continued to hum her little song in the kitchen while the eggs cracked and the bacon sizzled.

XXII

Heart Liver Kidney

The rain came down parallel to the shiny, oily street. It was long, dark and empty, and an ineffective row of street lamps clawed by a million raindrops did little to dispel the stormy night.

Standing under the bus shelter waiting for a cab, Lilly looked rigid, and it was not because she was wet. She wasn't. Very dry and very warm, for the thick, black overcoat was buttoned up, and the collars almost obliterated her face, Lilly might have been the envy of a bum who had shuffled in, shivering in the wet and huddling in the corner of the bus shelter.

She glanced fearfully at him, then up and down the gloomy street glistening under the rain, and finally at her phone clutched between fingers so white, they appeared to turn blue at the knuckles.

Quickly glancing over the message she had received a little while ago, she threw the bum a terrified look. He only muttered and huddled up. He didn't appear to have a phone, but under his great tattered coat, it was possible that anything could be hidden. Lilly looked back at her phone, and the screen light glowing on her young, pretty face was contorted in fear.

"Heart, liver, kidney," the text ran. "You can run, but you can't hide."

Even as she read it, the phone buzzed in her trembling fingers, and she jumped with a tiny scream.

"Lady, you okay?" wheezed the bum, shoving his hand into his pocket.

With a gulp, Lilly glanced at him, her heart in her throat. She turned away from his bloodshot glare and moved to the end of the shelter, where a spray of rain moistened her face. The bum watched her glance into her phone and grinned behind his shaggy beard at her white face and bug eyes. Then he yawned and cuddled into himself again.

The message on Lilly's phone threw her into a terrific flutter.

"Heart, liver, kidney," were the words again. "I am closer than you think."

With a moan of utter terror, she peered into the night again, snapping her head left and right. Then, deciding to run, she raised her coat collars as high as she could and splashed away down the street.

The bum watched her with one eye and chuckled.

Lilly's shoes were squelchy from the moisture in minutes, and her face dripped from stinging raindrops. Even as she ran, another message buzzed in.

"Heart, liver, kidney. Right behind you, lady."

With a sob, she turned once, her soaking mass of hair splashing about her face, and noted with a sinking heart that the bus shelter was now empty.

Was her mysterious stalker the decrepit bum?

Still, relief spanned her tense face because she noted two large, yellow headlights steaming under the rain hum up the street and slow down as they passed her. It was a taxi, and Lilly cried out in joy. An old, genial, and jolly-faced driver leaned out and asked her if she needed a lift. He opened the door as he spoke, and the young lady flew into the warm back seat.

"Not a night to be out, Miss," he said over his shoulder. "My missus back home has been texting me since this deluge started, begging me to get home." He grinned and waved his phone at her. "These gadgets are the bane of our times. Where to, Miss?"

"Um." For a moment, Lilly was taken off guard by the question because between peering out from her frosted window, hoping she wasn't being followed by the bum, and listening to the driver's idle chit-chat, she'd completely forgotten to give him her address. Calling it out to him with a shaky voice, partly from the chill of being wet and partly from her panic, she settled back and breathed deeply.

She was going home at last.

"Are you all right, Miss?" the chatty old driver asked, observing her in his rear-view mirror. "Relax. I know this rain can scare the life out of anyone, but it's only water. And you want to know something?" He snatched a smiling glance at her before turning back to the road. "Our skin is water-proof."

Despite her trepidation, Lilly chuckled, agreed, and glanced out the window again. The dark outline of buildings, gates, parked cars, and trees swept by in a wet blur. A figure or two huddled under an umbrella braved the rain as they scurried down the pavement like large rodents, trying to avoid the puddles of muddy water. A car or two sped by beside them, creating fountains under their shiny wheels, and her eyes scanned the dark interiors in those brief moments.

Another car swept by, and she caught sight of a hunched, bearded, and unkempt figure in the back. Lilly shrank into her seat as a pang of dread entered her. Was he the bum? Was he following her? At that moment, her phone buzzed again.

"Heart, liver, kidney. I am so close; I might have touched you."

She sat up with a start and tried to catch a glimpse of the car zooming ahead. Then, in a panic, she called out to her driver.

"Make a left at the next turn. The road is slightly narrow and longer, but I prefer to stay off the main street tonight."

"As you say, Miss," returned the old man gently. "My old woman has the same opinion, too, you know. She says there are too many crimes these days, so keeping off the main roads at night is somewhat safe."

"She worries for you." Lilly tried to smile, but her heart beat wildly. The car with the bearded passenger was ahead, so with the left turn coming up, Lilly hoped it would bewilder him and give her time to get home.

Once they had taken the suggested road, Lilly settled back in her seat, her eyes alert, scanning the dark tunnel of the road behind her for any following vehicle. There were none. Once, the old man spoke into his phone, sharply telling the caller that he was working and that the incessant messages and calls were getting tiresome. Lilly assumed it was the worried wife.

Then, after what seemed like an eternity on that wet night, the taxi stopped before her apartment block, and she stepped out into the damp, smiling gratefully at the cabbie. The rain had abated to a drizzle, but the cold sliced through her collars, sending a shiver down her spine. At the entrance to the foyer, the janitor rose from his seat and opened the door.

As she paid the cabbie, her phone buzzed again, and the light from its screen illuminated her petrified face. She glanced around at the janitor with a fearful sob. The message read:

"Heart, liver, kidney. I am at your gate!"

Lilly nearly collapsed as her legs melted to jelly. She turned and rushed past the janitor and into the lift. Even as the doors began to close, a wet boot wedged between the panels and the doors slid open again.

She smothered a scream. The next instant, she relaxed, admonishing herself for being so silly.

It was only the genial old cab driver squeezing into the tiny metal cubicle. A smile spilt his wet face as his nubby fingers tapped a message on his phone.

Hers buzzed in at that moment:

"Heart, liver, kidney. Guess who's in the lift!"

This time, Lilly swooned and crumpled to the floor.

XXIII
Behind Closed Eyes

Laiqua breathed deeply and closed her eyes. It was not so much to shut out the hubbub conversations and the folk milling around her as to delve into her own thoughts and space out, if even for a few minutes, until the next set of relatives swooped down on her to greet her and ogle at her wedding jewellery. They were all around, like crows cawing and feasting on carrion meat, fluttering from tables, descending on seats, bedecked, bejewelled and bedazzled by the lights, flowers and drapes of the wedding venue. Her husband was guffawing at the other end of the hall with his friends – a few last moments with him, they had jokingly suggested, before he became shackled for a lifetime.

As if a wife did that, she mused behind her eyelids glistening with gold hues.

But a few seconds was all she needed – her life flashed before her eyes, and the smile on her heavily painted lips crept southwards, freezing on her rouge-shaded cheeks like a boat capsizing in the sunset. A bubbly teenager emerging from the bath flashed before her. She ran, shamefaced, to her room, a threadbare towel soaking and plastering against her moist skin. Underneath, the emerging shape of puberty – widening hips, pert breasts and body hair. It was confusing, embarrassing, discomforting... almost humiliating. When she was eight, her uncle Karim Mamu said it would happen. With his gleaming black eyes twitching and his voice silky and soft, he'd trace an imaginary line from her cheek, down her neck, past her flat chest to the ticklish spot between her thighs. He said her body would change, and she would look like a bud in bloom.

He also said his cuddles and kisses had to be their little secret.

"Don't tell Bilquis Khalaah," he added, caressing her squirming little body. "She's my sister and needn't know what her older brother does all the time. Besides, what if she gets angry and beats me?" Karim's eyes twinkled insincerely. "You don't want your poor Mamu to cry, do you, my rosebud? And not a word to Nani, too. Understand?"

Laiqua didn't know what she wanted or understood those days. If she ran away from Karim's cold, wet fingers, he'd get cross with her and rap her on her knuckles with a foot-ruler. If she stayed, she'd have to squirm and fight his big, odious hands, prompting him to giggle and double his efforts. When Karim Mamu was pleased, his black, watery eyes twitched with delight and glimmered with glee. He hummed in the shower, and his voice became loud and vibrating under the cold water.

Those days, she adored Bilquis, her aunt and Nani, her blind grandmother.

Bilquis had looked after her when her own mother, Bilquis' older sister, had suddenly succumbed to a fever – the same one that had killed her father a few months prior. Laiqua, orphaned as an infant, had been left with a blind grandmother and a lascivious uncle. As she grew older, she wondered why Bilquis never adopted her completely. Bilquis was married and living away, but she had a remarkable skill of remotely controlling everything – from arranging groceries to bringing in help to cook and clean. Bilquis also took care of sending her to school; she controlled her education, paid her fees, and had her uniforms sewed. She did everything from the comfort of her home far away. She even supported Karim, who never worked a day in his life.

Then suddenly, Karim died!

Now, safely hidden behind gold-tinted eyelids, deep within her thoughts that no living soul could ever penetrate, Laiqua knew she could never grieve for him. More than that, she couldn't remember when her love for her aunt changed to hate and when she began to feel stifled by the walls of her home.

How lucky for that woman, Laiqua thought. Bilquis had rebelled and married a man of her choice and lived in an airy home with a garden and a white picket fence. She even had a cat! Now, if she had married a man arranged for her, he might have beaten her to obedience and kept her at home to cook and clean. Fortunately for Bilquis, she got to choose her husband – a quiet man who loved her and treated her like a queen but, in that same breath, cared little for the rest of them.

But Bilquis Khalaah cared, didn't she? With her eyes still shut, Laiqua smirked. Of course, Bilquis cared. She worked hard to disinfect a house sick with incest – she toiled to cleanse a dwelling crumbling under the patches of moisture that mapped the walls and smelled like stale urine even on the brightest of days. Of course, Bilquis cared. She knew all about Karim. She knew of the shadow peeping, the subtle touching and later, when a supple, fresh body emerged with puberty, the knocking on a bedroom door on some nights when menstrual cycles were safe! But it was easier to keep everything festering behind closed doors. It was easier to remain silent because, in a few years, Laiqua would be ready for marriage, and with all that had happened, Karim would naturally become the first choice for a husband!

"Khalaah, how can I marry him?" she had asked aghast when Bilquis, without blinking, had suggested that very remedy after the first instance of incest. "He is my uncle – nearly twenty years older than me."

"It's best for you," Bilquis replied impassively. "He's fond of you... and you will grow to love him."

"No!"

"Don't be silly. And don't be selfish."

"You married someone of your choice," Laiqua argued, her teenage anger rising. "I will not marry him, Khalaah, and if you don't put a stop to this, then I will, I promise!"

"Come, come," Bilquis replied soothingly, holding Laiqua's straining wrists to calm her down. "Don't get excited. "I was only joking. He-he! I wanted to see what you'd say. Of course, you won't marry him. He's your uncle. But look, your Nani is getting old. She needs someone to take care of her, preferably a young woman – you know, a daughter-in-law – and Karim Mamu is a great support. Don't you love Nani?"

"I do, Khalaah."

"And I know Mamu's been a little naughty," Bilquis continued smoothly. "He is, after all, a lonely man, and you being such a pretty girl, these things are bound to happen. But don't worry. I'll talk to Mamu."

Bilquis Khalaah never did, and the midnight trysts continued. Even Nani knew, for blindness brings on the sharpness of other senses, and her ancient ears could pick up the movement of even the neighbour's cat! Yet, between chewing her fix of beetle nut and fanning herself when the summer heat was unbearable, she pretended she was deaf when the bed-springs in the next room rhythmically squeaked with the moans of a man in his bubble of pleasure. So, by the time Laiqua turned eighteen, the ancient, smelly and mouldy carpet between the walls of her home, stinking of libidinousness, safely hid the many atrocities buried deep beneath it.

Then, suddenly, Mamu turned a leaf. In fact, he turned the whole tree, its roots, bark, branches, and dying yellow leaves! It might have been because he was diagnosed with diabetes or because his greying head was now showing signs of balding. Whatever it was, the eye twitches ceased, and he became a pious man, chanting verses from holy books, praying as many times as was needed by the catechism of his faith, decking himself with talismans, seeking wisdom from many wise men and endeavouring to grow a beard which, for some reason, never sprouted no matter what he did. Every evening, he had the disagreeable task of shoving an insulin needle into his thigh – once into this limb and once into the other. Oftentimes, he'd call Laiqua to administer the shot for him, and he'd caress her head and weep, begging forgiveness, but with his avaricious eyes on her young, velvet cleavage.

Out there in her home, which smelled of lavender or vanilla candles, Bilquis Khalaah rejoiced. With this 'old wine filling a new bottle,' she was set to make her next move on the chessboard of poor little Laiqua's life. With Karim appearing to become a better man, wasn't it now safe to approach the subject of marriage?

True, he was past forty, but wasn't forty the new twenty?

"I've raised you as my own, Laiqua," she told the young woman one day. "I don't have children of my own, and God gave you to me as a blessing. Mamu has become a god-fearing man – you've told me that the nonsense has stopped for some months now. Be a good child and say yes to that question I asked you years ago. Oh! Yes, I was in earnest! Your consent will mean lesser expenses for me and care for Nani – you love her, don't you?"

"You are mad, Khalaah! I cannot marry an old man!" Laiqua seethed and ran from the room, crying. What was Bilquis thinking? What?

Now, there were three reasons for this outburst. One was universal knowledge. Karim Mamu was comparatively an old man. In Laiqua's eyes, and they weren't shut as they were now while she sat on her marriage seat, listening to the humdrum conversation around her, forty was never the new twenty. Forty was a distended belly, man breasts, pencil legs and flabby arms.

The second was Karim Mamu himself – he filled her with disgust – his fetid breath, sweaty palms and greedy pawing when the lights went out; his repeated licentious and incestuous offences against a girl who was very nearly his daughter – Bilquis and Nani's closely guarded hush-hush! Though it had stopped now, the stench still festered behind closed, damp walls, waiting, waiting for the right moment. Call it a woman's intuition! Laiqua suspected this holiness was but a cloak he would cast off when the need arose.

The third had nothing to do with any of them. It was her little secret, wafting like a perfume of hope when Laiqua closed her eyes to sleep. The third was a young man.

Ayaan was tall, strong, and handsome, and he was studying to become a doctor. She loved how the sun glinted like a million rainbows off his eyelashes, how his neck vanished teasingly under his shirt, and how his buttons strained ever so slightly over his fabulous chest. He was perfect!

He was also forbidden! Her culture, where everything, including marriage, was arranged, forbade it!

Except in the case of Bilquis Khalaah! Now, if she had been Bilquis' natural daughter, would she have chosen an old man for her husband? Would she have been left to decay in a house reeking of depravity? Would she have overlooked Karim Mamu's paedophilia?

Bilquis Khalaah's appalling suggestion compelled Laiqua to run to her room and slam the door. Blinking her tears away, she shuddered from revulsion. Yet, deep in her heart, where a small hope beat for Ayaan, who loved her despite her brokenness, she knew Bilquis would never give up and would plague her like a swarm of locusts shapeshifting in the desert.

There was one way out, and Ayaan suggested it while they shared a soft drink in a small café on the other side of town.

"Agree to Khalaah's proposal," he said. "Agree upon the condition that they allow you to finish your studies. That way, you can ask for a longer engagement. Once this college year is done, we can take off together, marry, and never return."

It seemed a fantastic idea. But to never return? No! Laiqua wanted to see Bilquis' face when she married the man of *her* choice, Ayaan.

So, one evening, with a steely resolution, she rose from her bed, where the creaking springs reminded her of those nights when her uncle grunted like a filthy pig on top of her and approached her grandmother. The old woman was seated cross-legged on the floor, staring unseeingly at the wall, listening to ancient music on a gramophone, and breaking walnut kernels with a nutcracker in her gnarled hands.

"Nani," she said. "Tell Khalaah I'm sorry for being ungrateful. I accept the proposal."

"My darling child!"

"But on the condition that I finish my studies first."

"Why would a girl need to study?" the old brat asked, slapping her forehead in resignation. "But I suppose it should be all right. Bilquis would be fine with that. Call her number and give me the phone. I'll talk to her. You're a very sweet girl, Laiqua."

Nani couldn't hear a scowl, so she didn't see Laiqua's face twist into an ugly grimace.

Bilquis Khalaah, overjoyed by the news, whooped to her husband and shouted her thanks to heaven. It meant so many things! The marriage would entail no ridiculous expectations, and the expenses would be minimal; Karim would have a wife, Laiqua would have a husband, and her mother would have two caregivers – her son and granddaughter.

Assured that everything was falling into place, Bilquis began looking up travel brochures. She wanted to see the world with her husband, and Laiqua had given her that freedom! So, it wasn't surprising when she arranged a 'thank you' holiday to express her gratitude to her niece. With her husband, brother, mother and niece, she visited a vastly famous tourist spot in an equally famous land where the splendour and opulence of the city were only outweighed by the beauty of the stars that hung low over the desert stretching into the horizon.

It was here that Karim Mamu had a scrumptious dinner with his family, burped loudly to proclaim how full and satiated he was, signalled to Laiqua to get his insulin injection ready and proceeded to his hotel room to turn in for the night. He might have had other things on his mind because his eye twitched when he beckoned to his niece, but one would never know.

He never woke up!

Sitting with her eyes closed under her wedding finery, Laiqua blinked momentarily. Her hair was decked with jasmine, her eyes thick with mascara, her lips red, and her cheeks flushed with blusher. Around her neck hung gold, as it did against her hair, where it shone like a gilded moon crescent sailing a calm black ocean. A ring of rubies hung from her nose to connect to one heavy earring; upon her hands, decorated with henna, rings flashed like the sun's rays. Her garments were green and embroidered with gold thread, and her wrists jingled with bangles up to her elbows.

She heard Bilquis Khalaah sigh loudly in a corner; the woman was glum, silent and morose. On the other side, Nani stared at the chandelier but pontificated to a guest. Before her, an old hag of a woman limped up, admired her jewellery, blessed her with a foul-smelling mouth devoid of teeth, and hobbled away to the dining hall to eat her fill.

When Karim Mamu suddenly died, Bilquis' dreams came crashing down like a ton of bricks. Numb with bewilderment, she could only wonder what might have caused his death. The food? No! They all ate the same dish. Then what? The autopsy could determine no foul play and had stated irrevocably that the death was due to natural causes, but Bilquis' husband seemed to think otherwise.

"It's pretty evident, Billy," Laiqua heard him say one time from behind a closed door. "He killed himself."

"Why," Bilquis asked, utterly unconvinced. "Why would he do such a thing? He was looking forward to the wedding. No! No! The cause had to be his diabetes."

"How come there was no mention of it in the autopsy?" her husband asked cooly.

"The same way there was no mention of suicide in the autopsy," she seethed and broke down.

The memory of the chaos following Karim Mamu's sudden death twitched a delicate eyebrow on Laiqua's glistening face. Poor Bilquis Khalaah! She never tired of explaining what had happened to ten different shocked, concerned and sceptical hotel personnel; she fended off cross-questions from suspicious police, and she braved a dour-faced coroner to get a quick internment regularised. Laiqua recalled how she couldn't cry as Bilquis Khalaah did when they lowered Karim Mamu's body into the grave.

It was a nice spot where the desert bordered the land, where the stars hung low, and the moon bobbed like a lost vessel on the vast expanse of sky – a nice spot for a libidinous paedophile.

But now, even as that eyebrow twitched, a smile dawned upon her red lips like the sunrise over the endless desert. She fluttered her eyes open once, glanced towards Ayaan, and he winked back, his gold-lined suit and luxurious turban adding a royal touch to his handsome face. Running away and marrying him, as he had gallantly suggested, had been a good plan.

But she had had a better one.

She stayed and fought it out, using the power she had – the power that Karim Mamu himself had bestowed upon her – to sit by his feet and docilely inject his thigh with insulin while he ogled at her soft, creamy cleavage. Poor Bilquis Khalaah! So dejected despite the wedding! Now, she either had to give up her lovely home and move into a house of mould and decadence or shift the blind old brat to live with her. Either way, Bilquis' holidays abroad would exist, but only on brochures.

And what would Bilquis or Nani do if they learnt it wasn't insulin that Laiqua had meekly pumped into her uncle's thigh but a solution of potassium permanganate? Oh yes! It killed without a trace. Ayaan's medical books had given her the idea.

Laiqua smiled behind her bedecked, shut eyes and told herself that Bilquis and Nani would do nothing. Absolutely nothing!

Both had a habit of sweeping dirt under the carpet and pretending it didn't exist.

XXIV

Dressing for a Funeral

It's a universally accepted truth that a man who has just lost his wife must turn to his ex-mistress for comfort!

No, that's not entirely true, but today I will pretend. Pretend I can write as well as Jane Austin for one. Pretend that my intriguing opening lines are indeed a universally accepted truth; pretend that outside, it is bright and sunny when, in fact, the dull grey clouds seem as if a clump of sickly mushrooms are sailing a dismal blue; pretend my life is as beautiful as a sickeningly sweet fairy tale where magic rules the day and the love and warmth of a charming prince rule the night!

Today, nothing will dampen my spirits – not the rain-drenched sky, not my failed attempt to size up to Jane Austin, not the unpredictable turns of my life devoid of magic or princes and certainly...indeed, not the tragedy blown across today's newspaper headlines:

Woman found floating on city lake. Suicide suspected. Foul play not ruled out.

I cast one desultory glance at the headlines and fling the paper aside. Banal accounts of deaths and disasters are so common that I've stopped reading them. I like the crossword and puzzle section; I like to mull over the black-and-white boxes in yesterday's paper because the answers are available in today's. Cheating, I know. But whoever said I played fair? Life is full of deceit and pretend, and today will be no different.

Even so, the scoop would make an interesting read.

I take time to dress. It's a chore to look good, even if I don't feel that way. It's all pretend...very much like I want to pretend it's not drizzling outside and that poor Miss Austin might not be turning in her grave. But dressing is a chore! Why should we have to look good all the time? Shades, shapes, styles, fabric, fashion? Men have it so much easier! A shirt, trousers, a coat, maybe even a tie, shoes and socks, and they are all set for anything – be it a business meeting, a club night, church or even a funeral. If they wore the same coat or the same shirt, not a soul would notice. But if a woman were to commit such sacrilege – wear *that* same dress that she wore at *that* funeral ten years ago, the ensuing whispers behind maddened hand-fans would raise the corpse right out of the coffin if only to join in the conflab!

A man can go unshaven – who would care? A man could go *commando!* Who would notice? Who wants to notice? But look at us, I tell myself as I turn left and right before the mirror. The palaver! The layers! The plucking, preening and pruning – whether it can be seen or not! And for what? To be delectably removed one piece at a time by a bloke who cares little about fashion!

Okay, I think I went a little too far with that. My universally accepted truth might not go so far as to have my lord and master delectably remove my garments one piece at a time when he has a wife to lay to eternal rest and mourn thereafter for a while. But then, one can hope! At least I'll have the chance to bum a little dough off him and go on a holiday.

I think I'm going to need one.

I take time with the mascara. I realise my hand is trembling, so even though my movement is as delicate as a butterfly balancing on a petal, the cosmetic smears are thick on one side of my eye. I blink away the excess weight because I don't want to look too available to a man who has just lost his wife, Jane Austin-like opening lines notwithstanding. He is hardly going to raise his eyes to his ex-mistress when his children are swooping about, bossing over him and treating him like a two-year-old. I find his oldest daughter the most obnoxious of all. She hates me. Hates me because there was a time when her daddy preferred me to her mummy. Well, it's mutual. I'm not exactly in love with her, am I?

She's her mother's girl, and those are the ones to be careful of all the time. Mama's girls are tough and independent, and they take up arms at the drop of a hat! They don't stand for nonsense, are constantly suspicious and act as if they own their father, body and soul! And it's not as if her mother was any less. That woman – God rest her poor soul – was toxic, clingy and as biting as a rabid bitch. The one time I met her convinced me she needed to be put in her place.

I did.

The poor thing is gone now, and I am going to her funeral.

My hair doesn't look too good. Greying, rough, frizzy – even more so when I comb it. I pat it down, but the silver flyaway strands in the pepper halo remind me that I am only an ex-mistress – having to be content with a few crumbs thrown down to me from a bountiful feast. But then, I hope, not for long. Notwithstanding toxic mothers and possessive daughters, I have patented a universal truth, and if I am coy and sweet enough and extend my shoulder and arm to a grieving man, I might just be elevated to the position of wife and stepmother.

In your dreams, I admonish my reflection in the mirror.

My dress is not black. Though attire of any other colour would not diminish the fact that funerals are sombre, introspecting events, I decided that a fetching grey and pink dress would do nicely—small pink motifs on a grey background to remind us that from the gloom emerge pretty things! Round neck, puffy sleeves and somewhat tight on the top, it flares like an umbrella around my waist and looks respectable. Some of my belly is still visible under my body shaper, but I can't manage anything tighter. I might die of suffocation if I tried a smaller size!

The rain outside compels me to reach for my umbrella. It's neatly folded in its nylon sheath – a red flowering thing that folds like bat wings and becomes a compact lady's defence. We know that under those pretty nylon folds are metal spurs that can knock someone senseless – or even dead. A brolly such as mine is an effective and a veritable weapon. It fits nicely in a handbag and has quite the knock. Mine bears a slight dent from the other day when it curved around a head that swung too close to me. Would my brolly bloom in gorgeous red if I opened it? I might need to protect my peppery coiffure if it drizzled too heavily outside.

With suspicion and a tremor of distaste, I slide it out from its sheath and press a little button on its handle.

"Fizz-piff!" it exclaims, exploding into a giant flower above my head. Three spokes above me show signs of a small dent, and the canopy is slightly wonky, but otherwise, the brolly is good for today. I fold it quickly and sheath it. It's unlucky to open an umbrella indoors. I don't know why, but I've heard it's unlucky. I need a new one, though—one that is not so conspicuous in colour and without dents. A nice copper-yellow brolly, or maybe a teal blue one, will be a welcome change.

See what I said about women and colours? Men have it easy. Grey, brown, black, blue. That's it! Olive green if you're in the army. Khaki or navy blue if you're in the police. But if I were to dress in any of those colours, I would verily be asked if I were going to a funeral.

It just so happens I am.

I am now ready to leave to prove a hypothesis that has no base. My mirror shows me a middle-aged woman with signs of letting herself go. Hints - well, broad hints - of the little tummy are disconcerting, but the curvy hips are redeeming. My reflection has a youthful face with eyes shadowed by a touch of mascara. A fat right eyelash is proof that my hands aren't as steady as they used to be, and my image blinks in an attempt to remediate the fault. The cheeks are blushing, and there's a touch of lipstick that's not too garish. Framing all this is a mass of greying hair, and my reflection frowns. I don't like it, but I can't possibly do anything now. I'll take care of it later – once the rainy days are over and the sun shines through the clouds.

Because of the body shaper, my dress fits wonderfully. It hugs my figure around my breasts and swirls like a summer parasol around my ample hips. My arms are somewhat fat and white, like dough rolled into cylindrical shapes. My knees look like pink knots, my calves are strong and shapely, and my black shoes perfectly match my handbag. It's made of black leather and can hold the world, including a slightly dented red umbrella.

"Brollies are good like that," I tell myself as I turn left and right before the mirror. They, indeed, are, I admit again. A deft swing or a hard knock, and who knows, one might send someone hurtling off balance.

I reach for the newspaper and step out of the doors to walk to the bus station. It would be interesting to meet him again and smile at the astonishment bursting in his eyes. He is the epitome of discretion and would quickly reach into his pocket, pull out a wad of money, and send me off before any commotion began.

It would be even better to observe the consternation on his officious daughter's face and hear her rasp in total indignation:

"Daddy, I will not have a whore disrespect mama's funeral."

I have half an hour. That's enough time to read about her mother's body found floating on the lake and check if the newspaper got all their facts right.

XXV

No Returns of the Day

I can hardly recall why I had picked today to return home.

As it happens, I don't want to. I'm furious—that's all!

My watch tells me it's been exactly one hour and twenty-five minutes since I checked out and exited the airport. I know because I checked the time when I slid behind a Starbucks table to wait. With the last few pages of a paperback I'd picked up at Heathrow, I'm trying to make this coffee and two biscuits last as long as possible. Five times, I've tried to call the man in my life, and five times, I've hung up because the line only rang and rang and rang.

I choke up in anger. I hate waiting. But more than that, this is not how I dreamed I'd return home after three months of work overseas. This is not how I imagined I'd be received after sitting strapped to an economy seat with ankles like balloons on a flight that didn't seem to end.

It's already midmorning, and the airport is abuzz with people milling about. In trying to get my mind off my waiting and mounting anger, I absently wonder which of these people I would ever see again in my life, and even if I did, would I even connect that I first saw them at this airport? It's no use. I glance at my wrist to check the time and once more wrestle with my escalating rage.

Thousands of little trolly wheels from hundreds of suitcases glide by with soft, bumpy sounds over the smooth marble floors, aggravating the waiting experience. It's annoying to see families float up and down like ghosts, controlling or riding trollies packed with baggage of varying colours, shapes and sizes. With my back almost broken from heaving my luggage off the conveyor belt and lugging it out of the airport, I don't want to look at my trolly. More than anything, it reminds me of the two connecting flights I'd taken and the eighteen hours I'd spent over oceans and continents, deserts and forests to get here, to wait for a man who's probably forgotten about me.

And I thought I was special! The band on my finger tells me I should be, but I'm at Starbucks sipping cold coffee, dialling my sixth unsuccessful call and there is no sign of the man who has sworn to be mine, body and soul!

I could take a cab, I tell myself in resignation, but there's the idea of me, the long sufferer, at the back of my mind and the notion that I need to accumulate all my ammo to barrage him when I finally see him. I have to knock him down to a pair of shameful knees, put him on a guilt trip and compel him to seek forgiveness with flowers, chocolates and perhaps a diamond ring! Every minute that I wait longer makes my case against him stronger!

Yes, that rhymes, but I'm in no mood for poetry now.

I tear up. *Where the blazes are you? Today, you decide not to show up? To forget? I don't know which because you aren't even picking up your darned phone.*

A kind waitress recognises that I am in distress. My eighty-five-minute wait and my six abortive attempts with my phone haven't gone unnoticed. A few whisps of grey hair surround her kind, smiling face as she walks to me with another mug and two biscuits.

"Relax," she whispers. "He's likely on his way and caught in traffic." She's a pro at deduction, too, because she adds, "Maybe his phone died on him?"

"Thanks," I tell her, smiling through clenched, embarrassed teeth. She pushes the cup and biscuits forward and points to it with her nose. "It's on the house."

"Thank you, but..."

"Sush!" She orders, and age wins this battle I did not intend to fight. At least someone cares, I tell myself, choking up again. "Drink that and smile," she adds. "It's a beautiful day today."

I nod. It is a beautiful day. It's a special day. That's why I booked my ticket home today. Only I struggle to remember why it's special. It's not our anniversary, and my birthday was over five months ago. I don't dwell on it. I'm tired. I'm angry. I want to get home! The lady leaves me with her act of kindness, and I look away, embarrassed. The table next to mine has had churn — at least three different groups of travellers have slid on and off those seats. People are milling about on the polished floors, wheeling baggage, checking their phones, saying goodbye or greeting their loved ones. There's an excited conversation to my right, perplexity on the arrival or departure of some flight on my left and out there before me, a group of boys and girls are whooping "welcome home" wishes to a young, blushing slip of a girl.

They are celebrating!

Me? I'm celebrating two coffees – one on the house and the solitary act of waiting.

Then, at the two-hour and five-minute sign from my watch, I see him! He's hurrying from the car park and looks awful. His hands are mucky, and the front of his T-shirt seems like he's been wrestling with grease.

"My God!" I lash out in an odd mixture of anger and relief. "Couldn't you pick up your phone at least?"

"I forgot it at home," he answers ruefully. "Some of the boys came over for a beer..."

"You're hopeless," I rage. "I've spent eighteen hours on a flight. My ankles are swollen, and you were having a party with friends?"

"I also had a flat," he adds with an apologetic grin, and his grease-smudged shirt, grimy hands, and tousled hair make him annoyingly handsome. He takes my baggage trolly and wheels it across the polished floor as calmly and happily as a grasshopper, and I fume. How could he be so cheerful when I am so miserable? How could he not even think that there are words like *I'm sorry I made you wait* and *You know I will never forget how important you are,* and suddenly, I want to behave like a juvenile. I've earned it, I decide. Waiting for two hours and five minutes earns one the right to become petulant, even after a free Starbucks coffee and biscuits.

"Forget it," I snap and decide to cut my nose to spite my face. "I'll take a cab."

"What?"

"I'll take a cab home," I repeat, and in some corner of my mind, I want him to beg. "It's quite obvious that I'm not important to you." I snatch my trolly from him and shuffle away, and he bounds behind me, laughing indulgently. I know he's confused because I saw it in his eyes when I snapped at him, but his laughter now infuriates me.

"Wait, darling," he cries. "We were not having a party. The boys came over, that's all. I left well in time to pick you up, but I never expected to have a flat."

"Don't give me that excuse," I fume. "I know what happens to you when your friends come over..."

My phone rings at that moment, and I snatch it up. It's his mother.

"Where is that boy?" she barks. "Is he with you?"

"He is," I reply through clenched teeth. "He just got here to pick me up." I turn to my grinning other half. "It's your mother."

An awkward smile spans his face, and he groans, probably realising that she, too, must have been trying to reach him on a phone he'd forgotten at home.

She was because I now hear her declare:

"I've been trying to call him all morning. Would you give him your phone for a second?"

"Certainly," I hiss. "He left his back at home. What can you expect when his buddies come over for a drink?" I add wearily.

"I'm not surprised," his mother laughs. "But it's impossible to be angry with him today."

"Oh?"

"Please give him your phone," she requests again. "I'd like to wish my boy a happy birthday."

I freeze in absolute astonishment. Blood pumps into my cheeks and down to my knees. Mentally, I calculate the day and remember it is the reason for my flight schedule. My anger evaporates like water dousing a pan of boiling oil.

I pass my phone to him, a sheepish smile struggling on my cheeks. He takes hold of it, and my trolly, too, and expertly rolls through the milling crowd, laughing at something his mother said with my phone clapped between his shoulder and ear.

Eighteen hours of flying, swollen ankles, two hours and five minutes of waiting and a couple of coffees were instantly swallowed like a hard pill with a load of downright shame.

I meekly follow him to the car park.

About the Author

Cindy Pereira, born and raised in Bangalore, India, prefers to be called a storyteller rather than a writer. Her love for making up stories began at a very young age when her dolls became the actors for scripts written in her mind. This turned to writing in middle school when she and her best friend hand-wrote stories for each other, complete with binding and cover pages. Some of her stories spark from life events, and some are just yarns.

She loves to participate in short story competitions and has won several, both internationally and in India.

Cindy has a Master's Degree in English Literature and loves to trek, run and 'catch the sun.' She is married and lives with her husband in Bangalore.

9 7 9 8 8 8 9 6 7 3 3 0 0 3